HOUSEHUSBAND

HOUSEHUSBAND

AD HUDLER

BALLANTINE BOOKS · NEW YORK

For Carol

Many, many thanks to Jeanne Tift, Tom and Tricia Bass, Jean Reinhold, Mary Robinson and Karen Feldman for their loyalty and well-timed, constant vocal support. Also thanks to Nancy Zafris and the Kenyon Writer's Conference, which got me started on this path.

Thanks to Min Jin Lee, who gave me the idea for this book, and to Andrea Collier and Leah Barr, for all their editing, critiques and words of support. I also want to thank my agent, Wendy Sherman, and both Maureen O'Neal and Allison Dickens for their guidance and smart suggestions and thoroughness.

Most of all, I thank my wife and partner, Carol, for her patience and love. I thank my daughter, Haley, for her undying confidence. I thank my dad for self-discipline. I thank my mom for the spark that started it all.

HOUSEHUSBAND

This is a good day. Though it began as gray and sluggish as simmering oatmeal, it has steadily grown into an energizing, high-speed puree, ever since noon, when I got the phone call from Jo.

"Can you handle a dinner for five?"

"Who?"

"My boss and his entourage."

"Let me get my calendar."

"I mean tonight," she said.

"Tonight! You mean five hours from now?"

"I'm sorry. Can you do it?"

"Of course I can do it."

"Are you sure?"

"Of course I'm sure."

"I really can take them out, Lincoln, but it's Jerry and his group, and they always prefer a home-cooked meal. And they like your cooking."

"I can do it," I said.

On the drive to the grocery store, with Violet listening to a tape of *Sesame Street* songs in her car seat, I decided on an Indian chicken masala, which, after being thrown together, could simmer for hours with an occasional stirring while I cleaned the house. I'd serve it with basmati rice and some kind of cool, astringent salad that would cut the curry.

Jo had said the house was already clean, that it wouldn't take much to get it ready for guests, but she doesn't understand these things. It wasn't *dinner-party* clean, it wasn't clean like a fresh hotel room, everything aligned and pulled tight and poofed up, all the collapsed fibers standing upright once again.

So, with my masala simmering on low, I launched into tornado mode, like the Tasmanian Devil on the Bugs Bunny videos. I've learned that housework, done well, is impossible with a single-task mind-set. It's best to dart about like a hummingbird, tangential but still focused, conquering as you go, racking up little victories that accumulate and form something larger and significant. I began zipping from room to room, multitasking, occasionally peeking into Violet's bedroom where she played with paper dolls.

As the Lysol steeped in the toilet bowls, I watered all the plants on the main floor, stopping midway to make the bed in the master bedroom and pick up from the floor two pens and Jo's calculator, which I stowed in the pocket of my cargo shorts until I passed through Jo's office on my way to transfer the red load from washer to dryer.

Which reminded me: *Heat of a dryer.*

Which reminded me: *Dry heat.*

Which reminded me: *Dry heaves.*

Buy Mylanta for Jo.

Atlanta Braves.

Play date. Violet needs more friends.

As I dusted an end table, I glanced at my watch. Would there be enough time for the wine to sufficiently chill? I pushed three bottles of chardonnay into the ice bin of the freezer then set the oven timer for forty minutes. Before leaving the kitchen, I washed the floor in the main cooking area on my hands and knees, because damp mops simply redistribute the dirt into fuzzy lines.

I shook the foyer rug outside and draped it over my shoulder, then pulled out my pocket knife and snipped enough daisies and snapdragons and rosemary sprigs for a dining-room-table centerpiece.

Passing through the kitchen, I stirred the masala and called to ask the electrician to return on Friday to correct that flickering fluorescent bulb that made the laundry room look like an old black-and-white movie. The electrician reminded me of the light he fixed in the bathroom, which reminded me of the bathroom-wall bulletin board where we display clippings that amuse us. Since one of these guests tonight was Jo's boss, I found and pinned up the story from the *Rochester Business Journal* that featured Jo in the "Twenty Young Executives to Watch" issue.

All the while, I performed house-cleaning triage in my mind: The sandy front stoop—critical. I did not have to soak the knobs on the stove in ammonia water, not until tomorrow, but the backdoor throw rug with dried banana pudding either needed to be laundered or tossed into the closet. I could ignore the master bedroom if I shut and locked the door, but what if they wanted to see the house? They'd know we'd only lived here a year. Out of courtesy, women would request a tour, men wouldn't, but I couldn't be certain the group would be all male.

Make bed.

Cover Violet's pee stain with throw pillows from living-room couch.

Remember to call man to come shampoo couch.

New couch?

Property taxes paid first.

Call CPA.

C-3PO. Was Violet too young for Star Wars?

By five-thirty, I'd set the table and made the salad. Wine was back in the refrigerator, rice simmering in the steamer. I had time to pick five innocuous CDs that would allow for conversation but still convey to the world that we are eclectic and current.

At five to six, I was dressed and sipping a glass of cabernet. I dimmed the lights and lit the candles. This was the first time all afternoon I'd slowed down enough to notice my breathing and the beating in my chest. Though I'd taken a shower, my head was warm and flushed, fresh sweat beading on my forehead. I had that lingering glow from a full day of aerobics. Maybe I'd lost a few pounds.

Join a gym?

Buy birthday card for Jim, Jo's CFO.

Get Violet's portrait taken.

Check with dentist to make sure baking-soda toothpaste is okay for children's teeth.

I knew Jo would remember the evening as a success, though the details that created it would escape her. She wouldn't realize that a meal from scratch takes at least six hours, and that I'd magically done it in three. She wouldn't know that I vacuumed the seats of the dining-room chairs or oiled the squeaky hinge of the front door or played the CDs in random mode to help stimulate anticipation, but these things are important to me because this is what I do, and I do it very well.

Linc's Tame-and-Easy Masala

SERVES SIX

This is a good dish to try on people who are wary of Indian food. It tastes more like a cross between Indian and Mediterranean cuisine.

½ cup vegetable oil
1 tablespoon cumin seeds
½ stick cinnamon
7 cardamom pods (Any variety is fine, but I like the large black pods; they have a deep, smoky flavor.)
½ teaspoon peppercorns
8 ounces onions, chopped
9 cloves of garlic, chopped

3 tablespoons minced ginger

3 big tomatoes, chopped

3 pounds skinned chicken thighs (Don't even think of using white meat; it's dry and tasteless in this and most other recipes.)

⅓ cup plain yogurt

Salt and pepper to taste

1 teaspoon garam masala (This can be bought, already made, in any Asian market. It's not a critical ingredient, but it does add some life to the sauce.)

Heat the oil in a big pan over medium heat. Put in the cumin, cinnamon, peppercorns and cardamom and stir a few seconds before adding the garlic, ginger and onions. Stir a few more minutes, then put in the tomatoes and chicken. Add a few shakes or pinches of salt and fresh ground pepper. Mix together and bring to a boil, then cover, reduce heat to low and let simmer for an hour. Add the yogurt and garam masala, stir and serve over basmati rice.

The snow in western New York rarely falls with fury. With little to no wind, it coasts downward in wet, almond-sized flakes that pile up like dust on top of a tall armoire. Jo and I call it Perry Como snow because it looks like the fake snow on Christmas-season TV specials, the flakes a little too large, the path too vertical and ambience too serene, though there's nothing serene about the quantity. Seventy-eight inches fall each winter.

Obviously, as native Californians, we've had trouble adjusting to this, but our great house has helped. It is an Eden for indoor tropicals. Her entire minimalist interior is painted the same cool, light gray. Floors are either gray carpet, light maple wood or gray tile, all matching one another. And the best feature: Seventy-two windows! No curtains on any of them, just thin blinds that hide at the top of each bleached-birch frame. The main living space of the house, the kitchen and great room, has a ceiling twenty-two feet tall with three rows of windows reaching toward the top, giving a lofty, cathedral feeling (Bauhaus meets Notre Dame) when the sun pours through, which isn't very often because this is western New York.

I soon learned that in wintry climates one must bring

nature inside, so I've begun buying plants, which I frequently move from spot to spot, trying to create corners
that resemble dense rain forest with different species ran-
domly mixed together. My favorite is a blue passion flower
vine, *passiflora caerulea,* which I set in front of an east window in the dining room.

"You got a greenhouse?" asked the man at the nursery.

"No."

"That won't grow inside a normal house," he said.

"It will," I replied.

"There's not enough light."

"You're wrong," I said. "I know these things."

"Suit yourself."

Aggressive and beautiful, the plant twisted and climbed
eleven inches in the first two weeks.

As unconfident as I sometimes feel these days, I still am
self-assured when it comes to botany. I used to be landscape architect for the stars, both the has-beens and the
current pop icons. It was an exhausting job, continually
battling the misguided aesthetics of the nouveau riche.

In my line of work you learn very quickly that most
people don't know anything about the delicate imbalances
that create beauty. They try to color-coordinate flowers as
they would their clothes and jewelry, and they almost always plant too many. They use flowers as the medium for a
paint-by-number landscape, turning their yard into something that looks like an amusement park entrance with
dense, undulating swaths of daffodils, tulips and petunias,

the Muzak of the plant world. I tried to tell my clients that
flowers were intended to be random, dropped into place by
birds and the wind. Flowers should be an occasional, visual
surprise, like a found conch shell on the beach. But my
clients didn't always listen, even though they paid me the
highest landscape consulting fee in southern California. I
gave them my advice then moved out of the way.

My turning point—that imagined "click" that made it
possible for me to leave my job and enter domestic servi-
tude in upstate New York—was an argument with a client
in Santa Barbara, a sitcom star whom I will not identify.
She wanted white-blooming vinca to cover the entire
round expanse in the middle of her circular driveway.

"You don't want that much vinca," I told her.

"I want the whole thing white," she said.

"Like wall-to-wall shag carpeting," I replied, hoping
she'd understand my oblique reference to tackiness.

"Yeah, like white shag carpeting."

I did as she wished with one twist: Among the sea of
white blooms, I planted off center one basketball-sized
spot of red vinca, replicating the trademark mole this ac-
tress had on her left cheek.

She returned home from errands just as we were finish-
ing up. "What the hell is that in the vinca?" she asked.

"A creative touch for a creative artist such as yourself,"
I said, lying.

"Well it looks like hell. I want you to change it."

"I wish you'd think about it."

"I want it changed, okay? And I want it changed now. I'm having a party tonight. What the hell am I paying you for anyway?"

I sent Carlos back to the nursery for another flat of the white because I had to leave; Maria, our nanny, had a doctor's appointment at six o'clock, and I needed to relieve her. Because I owned my own business and had more control of my schedule, I was the fallback when Maria was gone.

Jo's red Saab was sitting under the carport when I arrived. She'd come home early with the news that would uproot and transplant us to the East Coast.

"You're actually home before dark," I said, walking into the kitchen.

"Smart-ass."

"Where's Maria?"

"I sent her on."

Violet was sitting on the floor beside the open pantry, arranging anchovy tins into something that looked like a miniature Stonehenge.

"Hi, Daddy. I'm making a house," she said.

"Very cool, sweetheart."

I kissed her on the cheek then sat down at the table with a bottle of Evian and started venting to Josephine about my day, the genius of the vinca mole and the ungrateful, ignorant reaction of my unenlightened client. "I'm ready to quit and sell pansies at Home Depot," I said.

Jo had grown silent, as she usually does whenever I jettison into geyser mode. She's great about letting me shoot off and usually steps back into the conversation once the steam has dissipated and normal pressure has been restored. In my Christmas stocking last year she gave me a key chain that says "I don't belch. I don't fart. Therefore if I don't bitch I'll explode."

Finally, I ran out of words, leaned back and took a drink of water. Jo reached out for my hands on the table and covered them with hers.

"Then how would you feel about moving?" she asked.

"Jo!"

"Jerry called me today. Something's come open."

"Where? Outside L.A.?"

She hesitated, then spoke.

"Actually, Rochester, New York."

I started to speak, but Jo interrupted. "I can say no," she quickly inserted. "I can tell them I want to wait for something to open up closer to home. I'll get another chance."

"Those jobs don't come open every day, Jo, you know that. You've got to take it."

"And what about you?"

"They have yards in Rochester," I said. "I'll start over. I'm sure I'm light-years ahead of them in design."

"I know you too well, Lincoln. I'm not trusting the sincerity of your response here. Six months from now I don't want to hear how I forced you to sell out and move. I don't want any of your martyr bullshit."

"I promise, Jo. You've caught me on the perfect day. I am so ready for a change."

And I was, at least a temporary change. My business, thirty-five employees and six trucks, had grown too large and was no longer fun. I hated managing people, I was terrible at it, and I ended up paying too much in Christmas bonuses because I felt guilty for losing my temper and saying awful things.

No one does things exactly the way I want them to. No one ever has. It's a problem they have.

"Daddy?"

"Daddy?"

"Daddy? Know what, Daddy? . . . Daddy? Know what?"

On some days my daughter talks so much it sends me over the edge. Violet is a precocious communicator, verbal enough that our pediatrician called in a linguist to study her unusually rapid speech development. People are always surprised when they discover she's only three.

Violet feels she must share with me every electrical occurrence in her brain, following me through the house to explain unnecessary details as would a bored, retired engineer. This is okay for a day or two, but it has a cumulative effect. If I don't get a Saturday of relief from Jo, I explode some time on Monday, which is today.

"Know why I like this baby doll, Daddy? Her hair is white, white, white, and her dress, I like her dress pink, pink, I like her dress. . . . Daddy, you like her dress? Daddy? Daddy? . . . Daddy?"

"Jesus, Violet! What! What, what, what, what, what!"

And then, as fast as toast pops up, the guilt hit me, and I hopped on that too-familiar, nightmarish carousel of self-flagellation: I'm a terrible parent. I'm lacerating her self-esteem. Am I not showing enough patience and love? Is this why she seems so needy? Am I too depressed to be tuned in? Violet's such a pleaser; is she afraid of me? What's wrong with me? Am I a bad father? I'm a bad father.

I'm experiencing one of those moments of burnout, actually periods of overload, when I slam shut the door in my mind that says "adults only." I try to hide behind this door, yet Violet keeps knocking and knocking and knocking to get inside. She's always there, following me, even when I'm alone in the car. She's a phantom, much like the feeling an amputee has about a lost arm or leg: I know it's there, I *feel* it. Oh, it's not there, sir . . . it's your imagination . . . But you don't understand, she *is* there, can't you see her? Can't you feel her? She won't leave me alone! Can't you make her leave me alone?

I plugged my ears. If I let her in I knew I would lose my mind, and when I regained my senses I would find a dead child lying on the floor.

"Here," I said, snatching the clicker off the ottoman. "Watch some television."

Just for half an hour, I convinced myself. But one episode of *Barney* melted into *Mr. Rogers*, which melted into *Sesame Street*.

I tried to lose myself in mail-order catalogs, but the guilt had already seeped in like a persistent fog. If I was going to be a lousy parent, at least I could have a clean house, so I grabbed the cleaning basket from under the sink and headed upstairs.

I was half-naked, wearing only a rolled bandana around my forehead and cutoff blue jeans splattered with a ten-year history of paint, when I heard the doorbell. I ignored the first ring, then the second, but finally succumbed on the third.

"Marilyn Zentino," said the woman with short brown hair, thrusting her hand out with Realtor confidence. "Tudor with purple door, two houses down. Welcome to the neighborhood." Slick and shiny with sweat from exercise, she wore red spandex tights and a runner's halter top that squished her breasts together like two water balloons in a plastic grocery bag. She smelled of fabric softener and a musky perfume in its sunset stage.

"Linc Menner," I replied.

"Like sausage?"

"Lincoln."

I apologized for looking so bad, that I was cleaning the upstairs bathrooms when she rang. I turned and motioned with my chin to the white toilet-bowl brush that jutted from the back pocket of my shorts like a dislocated bone. I'd used my T-shirt earlier to soak up a spill of Mr. Clean on the bathroom floor.

"I saw your wife's picture in the newspaper," she said. "That is your wife, isn't it? The new president at the hospital?"

"Jo. Actually Josephine."

"And you just have the one little girl?"

"Violet. And you?"

"Dax and Sarah. They're six and four."

"Where are they now?"

"I lock them in with a video when I go running."

"By themselves?"

"The alternative is murder. You wouldn't understand—you've got just the one."

"I'm sure it's different."

"Do you work at home?"

"No, no, just for the move. I'm a landscape architect."

She tugged at the bottom of her stretchy top. Was she trying to cover more of her skin or was it an attempt to draw my attention to that spot?

"I used to cater, but not much anymore. Steven wants me home with the kids."

"Steven in the green Cherokee?"

"So you've actually seen him."

"What's the uniform?"

"He's a pilot with US Air."

Violet had pattered up behind me and was hiding behind my bare leg. I could hear the tiny, spontaneous *pshh, pshh* of the air being pushed from the binky's rubber nipple as she sucked.

"This is my daughter," I said. "Hydrangea."

Violet smiled beneath the binky, peeking at the visitor.

"Actually, it's Snapdragon," I said. "If you squeeze the ends of her you can make her mouth move."

Violet, who for some reason cannot stand things being mislabeled, suddenly pulled the plug from her face: "It's Violet, Daddy! My name is Violet!"

"But you're not purple," I said.

"I'm not purple, I'm Violet! My name is Violet Anna Menner!"

"How old is she?" Marilyn asked.

"Three."

"Wow. Early talker."

She looked over her shoulder, toward her house. "I need to go pull the kids apart," she said. "Call me if you need anything. I'm locked in my tower here most of the day."

I watched her run across the grass. Toned, caramel-colored calves, dark for June in upstate New York. Did she lie in the sun? Did she go to a tanning booth?

I felt a mosquito land on my stomach, which was beginning to gain in mass like a rising loaf of bread since I'd been home with Violet. I slapped the bug, brushed the fleck of blood and tiny mangled body from my skin then reached down, picked up the carcass and stuck it in my pocket because I remembered I'd just vacuumed the day before.

I have this bad habit of judging people in the grocery store. It's one of those my-cart-looks-healthier-than-your-cart kind of things. I feel superior to shoppers whose carts are laden with the colorfully packaged foods seen in the Sunday newspaper coupons. I call these people aisle trawlers. As they unload their Pop-Tarts and Cheez Whiz and Lean Cuisines and jars of premade spaghetti sauce, I want to say, "Hey, look in here, in my cart. *This* is food: escarole and dried morel mushrooms, papayas, Stilton cheese and a naked baguette of sourdough bread." Jo says this arrogance comes from four years of working part-time in college as a kitchen helper in a fusion restaurant. In such an environment, food snobbery was equaled in strength only by fresh ginger and minced habaneros.

Good cooks know that nearly everything you need in a grocery store sits away from those middle aisles—produce, bakery, meats and dairy almost universally line the perimeter, no matter what city or chain. It's as if God, wanting to separate all his pure creations from the man-made concoctions, threw the contents of a supermarket into a spinning centrifuge, and all that was good and pure shot out to the edge, and all that was vulgar and superfluous remained in the center. The only time one needs to dip into the interior of the store is for a spice or bag of nuts. Or cat food or tampons.

I've always been the cook in our house, and this has made my job here much easier. Jo hates the kitchen, always has. In high school she successfully petitioned the school board to abolish the home-ec requirement for girls. Raised in a farming town in the Central Valley, she saw cooking as a trap. In her mind, girls who could cook married local farm boys and subsequently ended their lives at age eighteen.

I am less certain about housework. It is more like baking than cooking, with time-tested, measured ways of achieving results. For this reason, I talk to my mother on the phone sometimes two or three times a day. She complains about Dad's cigar smoke. I ask her why a girl's shoe size is different from the sock size. My Domestic Dear Abby, she knows the answers to all my questions: How much Clorox is too much? How can I get chewing gum out of hair? (Who would have guessed peanut butter?) She gives me pep talks about patience and sacrifice. I bitch about how I'm working my ass off in this house and no one seems to notice or care.

"Get used to it," she said. "Besides, I'm coming out to help."

"No, Mom, I can manage."

"You've never moved cross-country, and Jo's too busy to help."

"I'm not going to be doing this for much longer," I said. "I'm looking for a nanny."

"I'll help you find one."

"Mom, that's okay."

"I want to get out of the house, Lincoln. I'm ready to kill your father."

"What happened?"

"I don't want to go into it."

"Stay home, Mom, I'm okay. Who would cook for Dad if you left?"

"Your dad's happy eating shredded wheat. He could eat shredded wheat every day, every meal, for the rest of his life if he had his way."

I love my mom, but she's got an intense, penetrating presence, like maximum-volume Beethoven, and it gets tiring in person. She's best consumed in comfortably timed morsels.

I thought I'd successfully convinced her to stay at home, and had started describing to her a cute Violet moment from that morning, when Jo walked in. Seven-thirty, early for her. I hadn't even started dinner.

As I finished my conversation, about another ten minutes, Jo lingered in the kitchen, scavenging through the refrigerator, opening and shutting cupboard doors, setting a glass on the counter, all a little louder than necessary. The message was obvious, but I ignored it and finished my phone call.

When I hung up I poured her a glass of chardonnay and

sat down across the table from her. "You're mad at me, aren't you?" I asked.

"I'm not mad."

"Then you're disappointed."

She took a sip of wine. "It would be petty to mention it. I'd be embarrassed."

"Go ahead," I said.

"You sure?"

I nodded.

"Okay . . . I have this fantasy of walking into the house and having everyone happy to see me, and having everyone drop what they're doing so they can walk up and kiss and hug me because they've missed me all day. Instead, Violet's in her room, coloring. And you're on the telephone. You're always on the telephone."

"I'm connecting with the adult world," I said. "You're out there all day with real people and I'm stuck here at the kiddie carnival. It's my lifeline to sanity. I'm not a housewife, Jo. Don't expect the Ozzie and Harriet show here."

"Don't snap at me like that, Lincoln. You look like a Venus's-flytrap, and I don't deserve it."

I pulled the dish towel from my shoulder and started wiping the already clean table.

"You're right, I'm sorry. . . . But, Jo, you're out there all day with all those nice lunches and people to talk to and plenty of stimulus."

"An overload of stimulus, thank you."

She rested her elbows on the table, closed her eyes and started rubbing her temples with her fingers in little circles.

I was certain she had no idea why she was doing this, why she was mimicking an Excedrin commercial. Jo doesn't really think much about the seeds and germinations of actions. My wife is successful because she does not get distracted or frightened in a storm, be it emotional or meteorological, but rather bolts right on through—nuance, be damned!—like a runaway engine of a train. She frequently does not notice when I get my hair cut or hang another picture that I've unpacked and brought in from the garage. She does not know when we change brands of toothpaste.

Still, I could tell this new job had been a stretch for her. Though this hospital was smaller than the one in California, the move from chief financial officer to chief operating officer more than quadrupled her responsibilities. Everything under the roof of Genesee Memorial, including all nineteen-hundred employees and six-hundred-some patients, was her responsibility. Add to this the civic responsibilities that come from being the head of one of the largest employers in Rochester. Like Captain Kirk, she rarely smiles. It's as if all the worries pile up heavy inside her head, weighing down the corners of her mouth so they can't be lifted upward anymore.

My move here, to Rochester, might have been easier if Jo had come with me. I mean the Jo I remember from the past, not the Jo who is overwhelmed in this monster job. Not one to normally revisit the past, I lately have been reminiscing, recalling our travels together before Violet was born, to Central America, where we'd made an impressive

dent in our quest to kayak all or part of every navigable
river in that small-intestine-shaped line of tiny countries.
At dusk, when we camped, Jo would sketch the silhouettes
of hills and mountains then turn these on their sides and
name them as a famous person. She said every human
profile in the world could be found in the outline of the
earth's crust. On the day that I met her, when I'd gone to
the hospital to complain about a late landscaping payment,
I was immediately taken by the two framed linear drawings
on her wall, craggy but impressive likenesses of Jimmy Du-
rante and O. J. Simpson.

When Jo gets home I smother her like a dog who's been left
alone all day in the house. Sometimes, if I've finished making dinner, I meet her at the door that leads to the garage
then I follow her all the way to the bedroom, yapping the
whole way, downloading into her all the minutia from my
day of dealing with our daughter and the new house. I
know it's not a good thing to do. I know that I am most
likely pushing her even further away, but I can't help myself. Just as a mosquito bite screams to be scratched, I have
this burning need to connect.

I report what Violet ate for lunch and snacks and how
she napped and what she said. I give her details of the mail
and my dealings with the tax assessor and the grape-juice
stain in the carpet that finally came out after forty minutes,
forty minutes, of labor. I recount every conversation I had

with any serviceman who'd been in the house since she left that morning and any victories I might have won in bartering a better deal.

We'd been having termite problems. I discovered them when I was vacuuming in the downstairs bathroom and bumped into and crashed through a paperlike wall of beige paint on the baseboard. Treating termites is like painting over the knots in pine; several attempts are required. As a result, I'd grown familiar with Anthony of Tops Pest Control.

"Did you know he's been to see *Phantom* in Toronto three times?" I asked as she changed from her work clothes into jeans and a casual, beige, V-necked sweater.

"Yeah?"

"Don't you think that's interesting?"

"What?"

"That a blue-collar guy would drive a hundred and fifty miles to see a Broadway show?"

"No, Linc, I don't." Her head popped through the neck hole of the sweater. "What I think is that you're depressed and you need to get out of the house and meet some people. Look at you. You don't even shave anymore. Some days you don't even brush your teeth."

"I'm not depressed," I said. "I'm busy."

"I want you happy, Linc. You need a job and some friends; you need to get out of this house. You're driving me crazy."

"I can't get out and find a job until I get us moved in."

She sighed then fell backward, onto the bed.

"Come over here and kiss me," she said, patting the spot beside her.

"I've got dinner sautéing on the stove," I replied. "Your job might be done for the night, but mine's just beginning, okay?"

I returned to the stove and stirred my pan of julienned red and yellow peppers, onions, garlic, and fresh thyme, all shiny with extra-virgin olive oil. From the corner of my eye I noticed condensation on the bottom corners of the window over the kitchen sink. This was more than moisture loss from vegetables; the humidifier was set too high. I would have to lower it two points before going to bed tonight. Already, I know this house too well, pathetically well. From cleaning her, I know the knicks on the banister and floor tiles as if they were moles on my body. I know every badly taped Sheetrock line that, as the house settles and shifts, threatens to break the painted surface like a geologic fault. I know, simply by the feeling of the air temperature, when the heater is about to click on. *(Aha! I was expecting you.)* I know the favored corners of dust, where it inexplicably congregates and reproduces like tiny clouds of cotton candy. I am fascinated at the inequity of dust distribution in a house, how some rooms can take on a powdery coating in a day while others will stay spotless for weeks. Dust! It was everywhere. Though dust had become somewhat of a foe during these past months at home, I could not help but develop a curiosity and respect for its composition and behavior.

My interest began months ago when I noticed the

inequity of dust distribution in the house. Why did Violet's bedroom need dusting just once every three weeks when the master bedroom and living room developed a fuzzy coating in two days' time? Over weeks, I experimented, closing and opening different heating ducts, changing the cleaning agent from oil to a simple damp cloth. Did a room make its own dust or was it invaded by dust from another land? In the dustiest of rooms, I sealed with duct tape the cracks along the bottoms of the doors.

Then, this past week, Violet and I spent an afternoon researching at the library, picking out both adult and children's books, then stopped by The Nature Company Store to buy a microscope. Our findings were fascinating. Thanks to constant air flow, every square mile of the planet contains at least one piece of dirt from every other square mile on the planet! The rooms with more fibers, from carpets and clothes, appear dustier because it is those fibers that act as the infrastructure, the framing, for the dust bunnies we see rolling across the floor like tumbleweeds. We discovered that the common dust ball has on average thirty-five different ingredients, mainly flakes of dead human skin and animal hair. Indeed, through a simple dust ball a family's identity can be revealed, its ethnicity and choice of food and clothing and pets.

My house has become a mate of sorts. We are intimate. I understand her rhythms and needs and seasonal swelling.

"Okay, you guys—dinner!"

Jo emerged from the family room with Violet. She lifted her into the booster chair then took her own seat. I set a

steaming platter—fish and vegetables atop a pile of couscous scented with fresh sage and finely grated lemon rind—
onto the table.

"This looks great, Lincoln."

"It's tilapia. Farm raised in Colorado—No, Violet!" She
had started picking up the fish with her fingers. "Use a
fork, please. You're old enough to use utensils. Remember
what I taught you."

"Which reminds me," Jo said. "How is the nanny
search going?"

Of course I'd had no time to place the ad. The laundry,
six loads of it, had devoured most of the day, and I ended
up having to wash the white load three times because I had
mistakenly slipped in one of my new red bandanas, dying
everything the color of pink wedding mints. The nanny
search? It will happen after I pick up the drycleaning and
get the two estimates for a new roof and grocery shop for
the weekend so I can make Jo's favorite chicken dish, the
one with dates and oranges and Moroccan olives.

Which reminded me: *Get on-line to research winter
vacations.*

Which reminded me: *Buy coats for the family at Target.*

Which reminded me: *Will I ever get a chance to browse
the salsa CDs at Border's?*

Did I have any marinara sauce left in the freezer?

Red sauce on a plate.

Redskins in the play-offs.

Why don't they serve peanuts on airplanes anymore?

A loss of cabin pressure. Do those oxygen bags really have

*oxygen in them or is it a hoax to comfort us—and just why
don't they fully inflate with air?*

Breathe deeply, I told myself. Restore normal pressure.
Again now. Good. We do not need an explosion of Lincoln
Menner at the dinner table tonight. I will be happy and
calm, despite the fact that my brain is shrinking, and I am
losing touch with movies and current events and friends
and all those things that can elevate and carry me beyond
this cyclical existence of white loads and tippy cups and
mud in the foyer and poopy diapers. Everyone—Violet, Jo,
our cat Tillie—wants, wants, wants, wants from me all day
long. Food. Clothes. Water. Clean diapers. Doors opened.
Backs scratched. Lips kissed. Soothing ointments applied,
both in cream and word form. It is no wonder I feel like an
empty tube of toothpaste by day's end. I've become so accustomed to energy flowing *from* me that even hugging has
evolved into a one-way encounter.

"The nanny . . ." I said. "I just haven't got around to it
yet, Jo. But I will. Tomorrow."

Jo took a drink of her sauvignon blanc. "Good. I just
want you to be happy. I know you need some help."

I spooned some fish onto my plate and reached for the
pepper grinder. "Then why don't you start tossing your
dirty panties into the hamper instead of throwing them on
the floor?" I asked.

GRILLED FISH WITH PEPPERS AND
SCENTED COUSCOUS

SERVES FOUR

1½ cups chicken broth (canned, instant, or
    homemade)
  1 cup couscous
    Zest of 1 lemon
  3 leaves fresh sage
  2 red bell peppers, julienned
  2 yellow bell peppers, julienned
  1 onion, sliced
  3 cloves garlic, minced
  1 teaspoon fresh thyme
    Juice of 1 lemon
  2 tablespoons extra-virgin olive oil
  4 filets of a white fish (such as snapper, grouper
    or tilapia)
    Salt and pepper to taste

Bring the broth to a boil, add the couscous and stir.
Take off heat, cover and let sit for 5 minutes. Stir in
the zest and fresh sage, then set aside.

   Sauté peppers, onions, garlic and thyme in the
olive oil. Stir in the lemon juice, then set aside.

Rub a light coating of extra-virgin olive oil on the filets, season with salt and pepper, then grill.

Serve the vegetables over the couscous. Top with a fish filet.

*Wanted: Intelligent, responsible
nanny to love and care
for our gregarious three-year-old daughter.
Car, references needed.
Call Linc, 555–9556*

I'd submitted a proposal for the new desert wing planned at Rochester University's Eastman Botanical Gardens, and my chances of landing the job looked excellent. Only three landscape architects gave bids, and I was the only applicant who had experience with succulents. Yet I could not even think of starting work again until I found a new nanny, someone like our beloved Maria in California, to take care of Violet.

My ad in the *Democrat and Chronicle* drew fifty-six phone calls, and I soon whittled the list down to five candidates, whom I interviewed at the Burger King about five miles from my house. Everything is five miles from my house. We don't really live in Rochester proper but in Pittsford, an inner-ring suburban village on the Erie Canal populated with affluent doctors and corporate-executive families hell-bent on making it look as it did in the 1700s. A subculture of

college-graduate housewives, all with the same wedge haircut, has organized and fought off not only neon and low-
income housing but McDonald's, Target, Arby's and Home
Depot as well. The only franchises in the village limits are a
Talbots and Orvis Outfitters. I have to drive ten minutes to
buy a pair of pliers.

I first interviewed Nicole, a second-year student at Finger Lakes Beauty College whose boyfriend brought her to
the interview. Billy, she pointed out the window, was the
boy waiting in the navy-blue monster truck with a back-
window decal of a little cartoon boy pissing on the Ford
logo. Nicole had an earring in each nostril wall and her
lower lip.

Number Two was Cindy, who said all the right things
but gnawed her fingernails down to the nubbies, far enough
that the flesh had started to round over the tops, giving her
fingers the look of well-healed, amputated limbs. Self-
mutilation, I thought. Too tortured.

Nancy was sweet and plain and unremarkable, the
equivalent of a pink carnation, with kids in junior high, the
Chrysler minivan, and a husband she met in high school. I
wanted someone with more intellectual spark, someone
who, if they ever saw a pet monkey dressed in a pink
sweater on the street, would say, "Isn't that interesting?"
instead of "Isn't that cute?"

Joan's life was so full of God that she used the word
"Lord" as a noun, verb and adjective. She also had tiny
rhinestone crosses glued onto the long, fuchsia nails of her
index fingers. I wanted something more secular.

This left Patty Baumgardner, a fifty-year-old freshly divorced mother who was living with her parents in Fairport, the next suburb over.

In the afterglow of her divorce, Patty had rediscovered her late teens. She wore tight blue jeans and sparkly shoelaces in her white Nikes. She died her black hair flame red and told me she used to weigh three hundred pounds.

"Look—this was me," she said, taking a Polaroid out of her purse and handing it to me. "I eat like a bird now but I still like to cook," she said. "You should have my wiener schnitzel and spaetzle."

She wasn't perfect, nothing like Maria, not even close, but I needed time to train someone before starting back to work. And the idea of coming home to an authentic German home-cooked meal sounded very appealing. I could take the leftovers to work with me and reheat them for lunch.

"Who was that in the car that brought you here?" I asked.

"My brother. He drives me everywhere. I don't have a license."

"Oh?"

"I never have, just never needed one, but he takes me anywhere I need to go."

"Do you walk a lot?"

"All over the place. I could take your little girl for walks."

Patty looked at Violet, who had been coloring in a book of fairies quietly at my side. Despite her attempt to look girlish, there was a masculine air about Patty. With beefy hands, a large nose and forehead with magnified pores, she reminded me of Dustin Hoffman's *Tootsie* character. An unusual scar, an inch or so long, ran above her lips like an Errol Flynn mustache.

"Would you like that, honey?" she asked. "To go for walks and see the birdies and flowers?"

"Birdies like Big Bird," Violet said.

"You like Big Bird, honey? Me, too."

"Do you have references?" I asked.

"You can call my momma," she said.

A bag of tiny plastic dinosaurs arrived from my aunt in Fresno, and Violet immediately started playing make-believe with them in the potted plants.

"Daddy, come play," she said. "Daddy? Daddy? . . . Daddy?"

I didn't have to cook that evening, and the hill of clean whites on the couch could wait until late because Jo had a dinner appointment downtown. And these were very cool dinosaurs, the name of each printed in raised letters on their underbellies.

"We need a volcano," I said.

"Yes! Yes, Daddy! A volcano!"

I found an old vase from Pier 1 and stuck a candle in the bottom of it. Then I started stacking books, in terraces, around the vase and covered all but the opening of it with a brown blanket. The vase was red, so when we lit the candle it gave off a hot, lavalike aura. Then we went outside and found rocks, and we set these and some potted baby asparagus ferns in random spots around the crater.

"Now watch this," I said, turning down the dimmer until the overhead lights looked like tiny, glowing harvest moons. In the dark, the candle crater looked like it was filled with bubbling lava.

The doorbell rang. I looked over and saw Marilyn and her two kids peering in through the long skinny window that runs the length of the door.

"Are we interrupting your witchcraft rituals?" Marilyn asked after stepping inside.

"Mom. Look at this! Cool!" Dax and Sarah ran over and peered into the volcano. Sarah ran for the pile of dinosaurs and scooped them up like jacks.

"No!" Violet yelled. "My dinosaurs."

Standing by the wall, I whipped up the dimmers, instantly changing night to day. The kids looked up at me, startled, like raccoons in the porch light.

"Violet, I want to see you in the kitchen," I said.

"These are mine!"

"Now!"

We exited the room, leaving Dax and Sarah to play with the dinosaurs, which they began to set in spots around the crater. Violet and I met in front of the kitchen sink.

"Young lady, is there a reason you won't share your dinosaurs?"

"Daddy, they're mine."

"I think you're old enough to understand this, Violet. I think three-year-olds understand a lot of things that grown-ups don't think they can, and I'm going to tell you this: It's okay to be a spoiled child, and that's what you are, a spoiled child. But the day you start *acting* like a spoiled child is the day we stop spoiling you. Understand?"

She nodded.

"Are you sure?"

"Yes, Daddy."

"Then what will you do?"

"Share the dinosaurs."

"Good choice. Now go play."

As we returned to the room, Violet saw Dax and Sarah having their way with her setup. They'd moved plants around and Dax had already dropped the brachiosaurus into the candle. Violet took a deep, shaky breath and said, "These dinosaurs are from my Aunt Dot, and you can play with them. . . . Please."

I walked over and stood next to Marilyn, who was watching the children. "How'd you do that?" she whispered.

"She's a good kid, I don't expect anything less from her."

"You want us to leave?"

"No, no. I need the company."

"Why haven't you stopped by?"

"Busy, I guess," I said, though I knew the real reason was that I never like being the person in need, and what I needed more than anything were adult friends.

"If we don't help each other we'll all go crazy, you'll learn that."

I knew it already. With Jo immersed in her work, working fifteen- and sixteen-hour days, my boil of adult-deprivation had broken open that morning when the UPS man stopped by with a package. I don't even remember how it started, or what I talked to him about for five minutes (Was it cloud cover? Snow removal? The way cars rust here in the Snow Belt? Something to do with wintry elements.), but I do remember him finally managing to break away, saying something like, "Yeah, well, that's very interesting. Gotta go," popping the bubble, leaving me exposed and embarrassed of how I'd used a fluid rope of words to lasso in a helpless grown-up. Jo was right, I needed friends. I could not continue to unload on my wife night after night, the words spraying from my mouth like bullets. I would scare her away, just as Jonna Moyer did with her husband. She was the wife of Jo's former boss, a woman who yapped on and on, so much that she reminded me of a Pomeranian when the doorbell rings. Jonna didn't think her husband listened to her, so she barked more and more, thinking he might start to listen. But the more she ranted, the more he retreated, so she ranted even more. Finally, he left.

"Is Steven in town?" I asked Marilyn.

"He's on a Gatwick turnaround."

"Want to stay for dinner? I wasn't going to make much, just for Violet and me. You like stir-fry?"

"You wok?"

"I'm a California boy."

Marilyn minced ginger and garlic, which I seared in a half-dollar of sesame oil. We tossed bok choy, napa cabbage and green beans with some spicy, fermented black beans and soy and a little sake to smooth it all out. Too hungry to wait for rice, we decided to throw it all over couscous. As the kids played with the dinosaurs, we ate our food and consumed a bottle of sauvignon blanc.

"What about a mango for dessert? I made sticky rice last night."

"Sticky rice?"

"Oh, man! You don't know sticky rice? It's dessert of the gods. Rice cooked with sugar and coconut milk."

"You're not going to believe this, but in all my years of catering I've never cut into a mango."

"Until now," I said.

I rolled the fruit on the counter to find the direction of the seed, then cut away each side, letting them fall over on their rounded backs and rock to a stop like overturned turtles.

"Here, you try this one. . . . Okay, roll it until you feel it rise on an invisible crease, kind of a rise. . . . Okay, okay, that's it. Now as you push through the skin, start feeling for the edge of that seed with . . ."

"Shit!"

Marilyn dropped the knife on the counter and stepped back. Her blood, juxtaposed on the mango's glowing orange flesh, reminded me of peach melba. I hurried her over to the sink and thrust the wound under running cold water. She had a small slice in the webbing between the thumb and forefinger. As much as I work with my hands, I'd never really noticed that silky bridge of skin, well hidden but essential, with a texture reminiscent of an eyelid or the inner folds of a vagina.

"Are you okay?"

"I'm fine, I'm fine. I'm just too drunk to be cutting any damn mangoes. Sonofabitch!"

I reached into the cupboard and pulled out a clean cloth diaper. "Hold your hand up, like this, until I get back."

When I returned with the first-aid kit, Marilyn was sitting down at the table. She'd finished her wine—and quaffed mine as well—while I was gone. I pulled up a chair and sat down in front of her, straddling one of her legs, then reached for her hand and slowly unwrapped the diaper.

I dabbed at the wound with gauze, then squeezed a pea-sized gob of antibacterial cream onto my forefinger, and I began to gently smooth it over the cut, the silken flap collapsing under my touch as I rubbed in light, small circles.

I'm-Hungry-Right-Now! Stir-Fry

Serves Four

1 teaspoon minced garlic

1/2 teaspoon minced ginger

1/2 cup onion, chopped

1 teaspoon sesame oil

2 tablespoons vegetable oil

1 tablespoon black bean paste (This can be found in any Asian market and lasts for months in the refrigerator.)

2 tablespoons sake

4 cups chopped-up vegetables. (These could be carrots, bok choy, any variety of cabbage, green beans, whatever is available in the vegetable drawer.)

Soy sauce, salt and pepper to taste

Heat both oils in a deep, rounded skillet or wok over medium-high heat. Add ginger, garlic and onion, then cook, stirring, until onion is soft and translucent. Add bean paste, sake and a few shakes of soy sauce, stir again, then add all the large vegetables. Constantly toss the vegetables so they are all uniformly cooked. The cooking is finished when the vegetables are at the firmness that you desire. Adjust for taste, using soy sauce, salt and pepper. Serve over rice or couscous.

"Lincoln?"

I was lying in bed, reading a Martha Rose Shulman cookbook on Mediterranean food, trying to unlock the secret to spectacular hummus. Mine was not creamy enough; it seemed almost pithy, like a bad apple. There was some missing ingredient. Or the speed of my food processor was too slow. Maybe I was not cooking the chickpeas long enough.

"Hmmm?" I said.

"Honey, I have to tell you something. And don't be mad at me. You need to hear this."

I set the cookbook on my lap. "What is it, Jo?"

She sighed and brought her hands together in prayer position, index fingers pressed upon her lips. This was a big one, though I could tell she was not mad, just frustrated.

"Lincoln. . . . Honey, you smell. You honestly, truly stink. Why are you not showering anymore?"

"I am showering."

"When? Three days ago? Four days? You're working around the house all day, you're installing lights and moving things around. You sweat."

"Why bother cleaning up when I'm not going anywhere? Violet's the only one who sees me."

Jo sat up, took the book from my hands and set it on her night stand.

"And what about me? I don't want to come near you anymore. Did it ever dawn on you that you might get more action if you didn't smell like dirty gym socks?"

She touched my cheek with the back of her hand, as if to check for a fever. "Do you think you're depressed?" she asked.

"No."

"You're sure?"

"No."

"Ahhh."

"Listen, Jo, I don't feel so good about myself right now."

"I know."

"And that's a new feeling for me."

"When do you get word on the desert-under-glass job?" she asked.

"Any day now."

I felt guilty for not enjoying my time at home with Violet. I love spending time with her, just not this much time. My mother had told me I'd go crazy if I did not stop treating child care like a landscaping job. "Do not have a goal in mind," she said. "It is the journey, and if you don't stop to enjoy the little treats along the way you will go insane." Yet that was not possible. She was asking me to change my personality. I am a schizophrenic mixture of both my anal father and artistic, tangential-minded mother. It's why landscape architecture made such good sense: create and implement. Create and implement. Until I finish a task, there is no stopping for unexpected diversion, no matter how pleasant and rare it may be. I return to the diversion when I am finished, though it's often gone. I miss a lot this way, I know, but I'm very efficient.

There was no doubt I'd connected with Violet; I now was the default comforter and distributor of all that a child expects. Yet my whole time here, at home, seemed very empty, like a flight from Maui to LAX when I have nothing to read and I've already seen the in-flight movie. As five-minute chunks slowly drop like obstinate turds, and the blue of the Pacific drones on, I get mad because I know there are constructive, important tasks I could be doing if I weren't trapped up here, waiting. I love my daughter, but staying home just doesn't feed me in the right ways. I'm hungry, I'm sucking on Tic Tacs when I want pork enchiladas smothered in green chili, but saying so would reveal my selfishness and shallowness and inability—unwillingness?—to emotionally intertwine with a child's personality as I've seen only women do.

"I know what you need," Jo said. She picked up my hand and set it on her breast. "You need this. . . . Go shower, Lincoln. I'll be late for work, I don't care. Violet's asleep."

"I don't have any rubbers," I said.

"We don't need one."

"What do you mean by that?"

She looked at me, cocked her head and raised her eyebrows in an uncharacteristically coy manner.

"Jesus, Jo! You're not talking about another baby!"

She nodded. "That window is closing, Lincoln. I'm thirty-six. We've talked about this."

"I'm in house-cleaning hell, I have no time to even get myself a haircut. I have no life! How the hell can you want another baby right now?"

"We always said we wanted two."

"I think I've changed my mind."

"Well I haven't."

"Well you're not home all day like I am!"

I got out of bed, stepped into my dirty khaki shorts that I'd dropped from my waist the night before and pulled them back up to beneath my stomach. I had worn them for ten days, maybe two weeks straight. The spot of marinara sauce from last week had turned from orange to dried-blood brown.

"Why do you want another child?" I asked.

Jo sighed. "Because I miss my little baby. I missed her completely, Lincoln. She's not a baby anymore. She almost seems like someone else's child to me—I just haven't been here to watch her grow up."

Her eyes welled with tears. She looked down and picked out the pointy end of a tiny feather that had pushed its way out of the comforter. I sat back down on the bed, beside her, and with my arm on her lower back drew her close to me. I noticed she was wearing her pro-choice

T-shirt with "Abort the Supreme Court" on the front and "Keep your laws off my body" on the back.

"I hate to say this, honey, but you should have decided that before you took this job. You don't have the time for another child. Especially now."

"I know," she said, hugging her arms, retreating to some place I was not invited. "I'm kidding myself, I know that."

She lay her head on my shoulder. I could smell the Aveda on her hair. I love my wife's hair; rich and blond, it reminds me of fresh sheets of pasta. Sometimes, when we're out eating with another couple, I just sit silently across the table and watch her, the way she leans her head back and laughs, moves her hair from her face with a sweep of her hand, the way her teeth and eyes and jade earrings reflect candlelight, and I want to leave the restaurant that second and lie with her, the two of us stuck together like slices of bologna, and smell the oils and perfume on her neck until we fall asleep. After eleven years, this is what I feel.

"Awake!" Violet suddenly yelled from her bed. "I'm awake, Daddy!"

I stood up from the bed. "Can you go get her?" I asked. "I'm gonna go shower."

"Awake! Awake!"

"Are you okay?" I asked her.

"I'm fine."

"Awake!"

"Sure?"

She nodded, slipped into her white terry-cloth robe then went to fetch Violet.

Later, after breakfast, I put Violet into the stroller and walked the four blocks to the subdivision park. Jo was right, I needed to get out and mingle and connect with others. Pairs of young mothers talked on two of the three benches. I took the third as Violet played in the sandbox. I nodded and smiled at the other women, but they ignored me as they so often do, hiding behind their dark glasses.

I looked around the park, pathetically landscaped with spindly trees no doubt placed by the backhoe driver himself. On the northern edge I saw a patch of some unknown, blooming weeds. Curious, I walked over to make sure I wasn't mistaken. I still was learning the flora of the northeast, and this could have been something new to me. Indeed it was, some sort of flowering ground cover, pale pink masquerading as white.

I pulled a handful from the ground and took them over to Violet.

"Pink," I said.

"White," she replied.

"Pink."

"White."

"Pink."

"White."

We verbally see-sawed back and forth until she broke into laughter: "Daddy, Daddy, Daddy . . . whiiiiiiiite."

I stuck them in the sand so they could stand on their own. "Baby trees," I said.

"Ohhhhhh," she replied, clapping her hands.

I began to build a model of how the park should have been designed and landscaped. Violet watched me, intrigued by this tiny little world I was creating in the sand. She walked about the park, gathering dead, brown grass and thick, waxy leaves from rhododendrons, which she brought to me. I made a Japanese bridge from sticks the size of toothpicks. I dug small ponds by lining the sand with mud so they held water. I changed the sandbox from a rectangle to more of a random cumulus-cloud shape, which wrapped around an imaginary, shady oak. I moved the parking lot to the far side of the park and planted a line of cypress trees to hide the cars.

"I wish we could be little bugs and play in this park, you and me," I said.

"You and me," she repeated. "Bug, inseck." In the past few weeks, new words had been dropping down like ripe apples from a tree.

"Hello," said an unfamiliar voice.

I looked up. It was one of the women from the benches, though I couldn't tell which one. They all look alike to me, these eastern suburban mothers, like a group of mule deer in a clearing. They've all got the wedge haircuts, the same pleated khaki shorts, the leather loafers or sandals, the same sleeveless tops, most likely Eddie Bauer plum or hunter green or black. They take great pains to camouflage themselves, though I can't figure out what it is they're hiding from.

Without even greeting me, the woman crouched down on her knee, took Violet's hands in hers and looked deeply into her eyes, as if she were checking to see if her pupils were dilated.

"Is everything okay here, honey?" she asked.

"Can I help you?" I said, though she ignored me.

Violet looked up at me, then at the woman, who asked her again: "Is everything *okay?*"

"Daddy?" Violet replied, pulling her hand from the woman's grasp and yanking on the leg of my khaki shorts. "Are things okay?"

"Yes, honey, everything's fine," I replied, turning to the woman. "Can I ask you what this is about?"

I knew immediately she had worked out the inaccurate equation in her mind. One grown man plus one toddler in the middle of the morning equals either, *A*: child molester with victim, or *B*: estranged father kidnapping his daughter.

"Your daughter looked troubled," she said.

Bullshit, I thought. I stared at her, saying nothing, waiting to see how she would craft a dignified, convincing exit from this situation. I refused to offer a hand to pull her out: *Oh, I understand what you were doing, and thank you so much for being concerned.* But I'd grown weary of women judging me everywhere I went.

"Are you new in the neighborhood?" she asked.

"Yes. Very new." I was cool and precise, like fingernails being clipped.

"And you are . . ."

"Linc Menner. And you are . . ."

"Mirabel Steiner. Have I met your wife?"

"Probably not."

"Who stays with your daughter?"

I did not like this woman, the playground bully who made me feel like an incompetent outsider.

"My dead uncle stays with her," I said. "I put a wig and a dress on him and set him in a chair in the window and pretend he's alive."

And I tried to smile like Anthony Perkins.

Patty started working for us two half-days a week, a part-time schedule until I returned to work. From the get-go, high-fat food items started disappearing from my kitchen, though she swore that all she ate during the day was a small green salad sprinkled with lemon juice.

"She's the nanny," Jo said. "She's going to be in your kitchen, Linc."

"I know that," I replied, "but she lies."

"About what?"

"About things disappearing. On Monday she drained half a huge bottle of safflower oil. I could tell by the smell that she deep-fried something, but I still can't find anything missing from the freezer. . . . And she's lied about the pepperoni, too."

I keep on hand a stick of pepperoni, which I occasionally use as a flavoring agent in sautéing, and in one day's time it shrank from ten inches to one.

"How could anyone chew and swallow that much fatty meat in one day?" I asked.

"She's got to eat, Lincoln. What's bothering you?"

"What's bothering me is that I asked her about it. I was even nice about it: I said, 'Patty, the next time you use the last of something, like that pepperoni, let me know so I can pick more up at the store.' "

"And . . ."

"And she said she doesn't like pepperoni, that she never touches the stuff."

"She obviously has some eating disorders or she wouldn't have weighed three hundred pounds," Jo said.

"Yeah, well I don't like her lying," I said. "If she lies about stuff like that she'll lie about other things, too."

"Cut her some slack, Lincoln. I don't understand your anger here. She's just started, and you've got this inexplicable animosity toward her."

"I just happen to care about Violet," I said. "Someone has to."

"I'm going to ignore that one."

The bottom line here is guilt. I do not deserve to have hired help because I am not working and bringing in money. This is my job, and I have to do it well, and I have to do it by myself, and because the job creates nothing tan-

gible (Translation: *Money!*), I go out of my way to let Jo
know how hard I am working. The only time I order take-
out is when Jo isn't home for dinner. It is important that
when she gets home I am clattering about in the kitchen,
sweating and fretting, because I have to show her that my
work here is as consuming and demanding as hers. Even if
I've had a good day I most likely will not tell Jo because I
don't want her to think that my life at home is enjoyable
and fulfilling, not even for the seven percent of the time
that it truly is. She cannot work harder than I do at home,
because if she does I'll feel like a slacker, guilty, guilty,
guilty. Lean Cuisines and frozen peas are out of the question. Jo says she wants to see me happy, but happiness indi-
cates a lack of struggle. I am earning my keep. A kept
man is happy, an overworked man is not. *I'm working here,
damnit! You think you're busy? Try on my shoes for once.* I'm
sure this is why I bitch so much to Jo about all my responsibilities. I am convincing her—perhaps myself as well—of
my worth to this household.

I want to like Patty, I honestly do. All this would be
easier if I liked her. The problem is that she has assumed
too much authority too soon. She sees herself as my savior.
In her mind, a man's place is not in the home, and she au-
tomatically assumes I'm incompetent in the areas of cooking, cleaning, child care and decorating.

"You need to get some nice lace doilies for those end
tables," she said.

"I like things plain, Patty. The room is supposed to be
minimalist. Beauty in simplicity."

"Well if ya ask me it's pretty boring. You need some throw pillows and some of those little rugs with tassels on 'em. Like at Penney's."

"Your job is to develop Violet's mind."

"I'm just tryin' to help, for chrissakes."

Already, Patty's child-care philosophy was too passive for my taste. She has a habit of sitting with her Danielle Steel book at the table, reacting only when Violet needs something. I want more than that. I want every waking hour to be stimulating or fun, always developmental.

"Take her to the library," I suggested. "Or go on a walk and pick up leaves. Talk about the trees and why they change color."

"We went on a walk yesterday," she said.

"So do it again. She needs to have active mental stimulation every day."

"She's a kid, let her play."

"So play with her."

Patty walked over to the sink and turned on the water. She has an annoying habit of rinsing an already clean sink with the vegetable sprayer, then drying it off as you would a wet car and draping the folded towel over the isthmus between the sinks. She does this at least twenty times a day. It drives me crazy.

"I wish you had cable," she said. "Kids love TV, it's good for 'em, educational."

"TV is poison, and it's a tool for lazy parenting."

"At least you could let her watch more than one video a day. How we gonna fill our days?"

"There's so much out there, Patty, just think like a kid. Go watch a spider for thirty minutes. Walk over to your mom's and let Violet make meatballs with her. Play in the sandbox. Have some fun, it's your chance to be a kid again."

"I don't know what your problem is with me, but you got a problem," she said.

"No problems, Patty, I just want you to do your job."

That afternoon, when I returned from errands, Patty told me she'd taken Violet out for a walk, but I could tell from a quick look in the closet that Violet's coat had not been moved, the right arm still situated where I strategically placed it, casually intertwined with the arm of the neighboring sweater.

"Did you put on her coat?" I asked.

"Of course I put on her coat."

"The pink one in the closet?"

"Yeah, the pink coat."

I will test her again. I will set a picture book on the end table by the couch and ask her to read it while I'm researching at the library for the desert project. I will pull a hair from my mustache and set it on top of the book. If I return and the hair is missing, I will know she has done as I asked.

For Father's Day Jo had given me a stapled pad of homemade "Love Coupons." They say things like, "Worth one fifteen-minute blow job," and "Good for one refusal of corporate-spouse appearance."

"I want to use this one for tonight," I said, handing her a dollar-sized yellow coupon that would pay for my night's freedom. She finished brushing on her mascara then looked at the coupon I'd set on the counter before her.

"Sorry, Linc. I'm not accepting that coupon tonight. This is a command performance."

"Why?"

"I need you with me. Everyone's spouse is going to be there."

"I don't need to be there. Why do I need to be there? I just stand there and have people ignore me."

"Lincoln . . ."

"Okay, I'll go, but I'm not shaving."

"Yes, you will shave. It's black-tie."

"I don't like this social aspect of your new job, Jo. It's not Lincoln-friendly."

Our biggest fight of the past summer had been over such a social engagement, the Fourth of July picnic for the

hospital executives and their families. Jo had gone in early
to work and instructed me to arrive with Violet at two
o'clock. Unfortunately, we showed up at six, much later
because I'd run into some huge maple roots as I was digging a perennial bed on the east side of the house.

I quickly performed marital triage in my mind: Do we
take another hour to clean up and miss the entire picnic, or
do we go as we are? I did manage to grab a fresh T-shirt,
and I got most of the dirt wiped off my bare legs. Violet
looked pretty good, not too much dirt on her faded, yellow
sundress, though I made the mistake of allowing her to eat
a frozen strawberry pop on the way to the picnic. Her hair
was a mess, I have to admit. I never know what to do with
Violet's frazzled blond hair, it's too long, so I stuffed it all
inside an old California Angels baseball cap that I found in
the trunk.

Jo frowned when she spotted us walking across the
courtyard, toward the grill where she was cooking hot dogs.

"It's a picnic," I reassured her. "Informal, right?"

"You're the spouse of the hospital COO, Lincoln. You
need to dress accordingly."

"I'm not Carol Brady, Jo. I'm not some brain-dead,
adoring housewife, and it's not my job to make sure that
your postcard picture of the executive family exudes perfection and prosperity. Okay?"

"You are an adult, Lincoln. Adults dress up for parties."

"But you don't need me here. I don't need to be here."

"Have you forgotten how many grand openings I've

been to with you? And I clapped and oohed and aahed over every hedge and garden like a good little woman. Don't you think you could do the same for me?"

"No," I said. "Because I'm not like that."

"And how hard would it have been to put some shoes on your daughter's feet, huh? Is this asking too much?"

"I'm very busy, Jo. I don't have time for these things."

"Then that means you don't have time for *me*, Lincoln. And that hurts."

This black-tie, the annual meeting for the Greater Rochester Chamber of Commerce, was in the ballroom of the downtown Marriott. We shared a table with the chairman of the Monroe County Commission and his wife, Natalie; the head of Rochester Telephone and his wife, Karen; and a senior vice president of Mohawk Electric Company who wasn't married. It didn't take long to figure out why. I'd grown accustomed to such assholes. Stuck in this position—me, at home with no socially acceptable job— I've discovered that such men often will smile but look beyond me as they shake my hand at a cocktail party or at the grocery store, watching the door to see who else is coming in because they think I have nothing to offer them, nothing interesting to say. My black friends say this happens to them all the time, that their white peers pass over them like footnotes at the bottom of a page, that in order for them to be heard they have to stick their foot in before the door closes then shove it open and yell their two cents' worth. I'm a minority, part man, part woman. Right now, with no job, I am Jo Menner's husband. I'm not sure what happened to Linc. Linc is drowning. That's him over there, that head of dark-brown hair under water. Would someone please go and pull him out?

Finally, unfortunately, he turned to speak to me.

"So, Larry—you don't work, right?"

The two wives at the table, my new friends, looked at each other, then at me, checking my reaction, and my first reaction to this asshole's question was to go through my chest-beating spiel—I'm a landscape architect taking some time off to be with my daughter—but the two stay-at-home mothers and I had been comparing notes on dry cleaners and potty training and produce sections of different grocery-store chains. They had praised me for taking time off to move and nurture my family, and praise is what I seem to hunger for most these days. I like women because they're much freer with compliments, and now I know why. They toss them out, like boomerangs, in hope they'll get one in return. Jo's not like this, she's very male when it comes to dropping comments of praise. I don't think she has any idea how needy I am when it comes to praise, and I didn't always need it as much as I do now. I work in a vacuum all day long, hoping that someone, somewhere will notice my efforts. I feel like a laborer hired to paint a mural on the walls of a photographer's cavernous darkroom, brushstroke after brushstroke in a black room that will never see light.

I could not abandon these two women. I would not be a

traitor. Society may expect women to be silent sufferers, but I could say what I wanted to and get away with it.

"I'm sorry," I asked, "but what's your name again?"

"Robert."

"You know, Robert, my name is Linc, not Larry."

"Yeah, sorry."

"And I do work. I run the house and the family so my wife is free to make lots of money."

"But you don't work full-time," he said.

"No. You're wrong. I do."

Karen and Natalie looked at each other and raised their eyebrows. Evidently I'd lost the cordial tone of my voice because all the other conversations at the table abruptly stopped. All eyes turned to the electric-company jerk and me.

"I've worked in the corporate world," I said. "I've also owned and run my own company of thirty employees. And I'll tell you what—this is the hardest job I've ever had."

"Oh, yeah—watching TV all day," he said, smiling, scanning the table in hopes of snagging others' laughter. "How hard can that be?"

Jo squeezed my thigh. I ignored her.

"You couldn't do what I do," I replied. "You don't have the balls, buddy."

"Okay, hey . . . Sorry."

His palms went up in surrender, but I couldn't stop, fueled somewhat by the three glasses of merlot.

"Do you know what it's like to be completely cut off

from the adult world? It would be like dropping you in the middle of a Chinese prison for five years. You could talk until you're red in the face, but no one would understand you, no one would listen to you and pretty soon you'd start to think you were invisible."

I'm certain I appeared rabid, even shooting a few specks of spit across the table. What could he say? How could he respond? He sat there.

"You want to know what I do at home? I'll tell you what I do. I'm creating a compassionate future leader of tomorrow. I feed and nurture a hospital president in charge of the quality of health care in this city. I help maintain relationships between families, the kinds of relationships that are the very safety net of civilization. I also have an excellent vegetable garden and I'm in the process of building shelves in the garage. That's what the fuck I'm doing at home, and I doubt you could do half of it. Now if you'll excuse me, I think I'm going outside for a walk."

As I walked past Jo, striding toward the door, I heard her say, "Linc's been under a lot of pressure lately."

She found me sitting on the steps outside the hotel. I'd taken off my bow tie because it was strangling me. Likewise for my jacket. How had I gained all this weight? What was it—five pounds?

"What the hell was that about?" she asked.

"You didn't have to apologize for me," I said.

"Yes, I did."

"He asked for it."

"He may have asked for something, Lincoln, but not what you gave him."

"I'm sorry. I'm a liability, I know that. Do you want me to go in and apologize?"

She shook her head. "I think a note in the mail might be better."

"I'm just tired of feeling like no one respects me."

Jo picked up my jacket from the step and sat down beside me.

"What about me?" she asked.

"What about you?"

"I have complete respect for you."

"I don't want your pity, Jo."

"Look what you've done, Lincoln. You've given up an incredible career to move your wife and family cross-country. You've single-handedly moved us in, you've refurbished a bathroom and built a deck, you've cooked nearly every meal for us, and you're great with your daughter."

"I'm great with Violet?"

"I can't believe you don't know that. You're fantastic. She's so happy, she's so stimulated right now, Lincoln. Her manners are impeccable. She does not act like the normal three-year-old. She doesn't even miss me, that's how strong you are. You are strong *and* loving. It's a shame you're not happy doing it because you're better than any child care we can hire."

"Yeah?"

"Yes."

I picked up a piece of paper from the sidewalk, looked around me for a trash can then stuffed it into my pocket.

Better enforcement of litter laws.

The crying Indian in the old television commercial.

More TV for Violet? Was I sheltering her too much?

The scent of a little girl's neck after playing in the sun.

Where was the mildew smell coming from in the garage?

When we got home, the baby-sitter, a sweet girl named Anna from Nazareth College, said my father had called and that I should call him back. I dialed his number with tethered alarm; my dad rarely calls without my mother on the line. I could think of two other times this had happened: when his mother died and the day he got word that Menner Ford-Lincoln-Mercury snagged the California Department of Health contract for seventy-five Crown Victorias. My dad is a good man with the focus of a famished lion. This means, unfortunately, that much of his life lies in the blurry field, and this gets him into trouble in relationships with friends and family, especially my mother.

"Hey, Dad," I said. "What's going on?" I could hear a television in the background.

"Have you heard from your mother?" he asked.

"Not for a few days. Wednesday, I guess. No. Thursday. Why?"

"She's gone."

"What do you mean?"

"The Town Car's gone. She's gone. I can't find her any-where in Bakersfield."

"What about Marion?" I asked, referring to my mom's friend three doors down.

"She hasn't seen her. . . . Did she say something to you?"

"About leaving?"

"Yes."

"She was thinking of coming out to visit, but I talked her out of it. She was pissed off at you about something."

"Pissed off?"

"Yeah."

"For what?"

"I don't know."

I could have given him a variety of reasons. My mom shares too much with me. I am the daughter-confidant she never had. I'm certain I was the only boy in Bakersfield who knew the words to "I Am Woman" at age five. We cook and shop together when I visit. When she went through therapy for the first time she called me to share the insights she gained about her and Dad's dysfunc-tional sex life. She tells me woman things I'd rather not hear. I don't know how many times she's asked for my dark glasses in a restaurant so she can ogle some guy without being detected.

"How long's she been gone?" I asked.

"I don't know—two days? Day and a half?"

"Shit, Dad! Didn't you call the police?"

"Don't overreact, Lincoln."

"You think she's been kidnapped?"

"For chrissakes, she wasn't kidnapped."

"What then? She ran away? An afternoon's one thing, Dad, but two days?"

And then, unflappable and unemotional as Julia Child, he said, "Just let me know if you hear something—okay?"

After we hung up, Jo walked into the kitchen. "Aren't you going to call the police?"

"No," I said. "I think she's okay."

"How do you know?"

"I'm not sure."

If I'd learned anything these past few months, it's that women's intuition is not a women's thing at all. Women's intuition is nothing more than senses on steroids. It exists because no one likes to hear a child cry or a grown-up complain. The caregiver must learn to scrutinize every motion and sound of a human, much the same way a seismologist monitors a smoking volcano. The eyes, for example, soon learn that the scrunching of the child's nose precedes the pursing of the lips which foretells a shattering wail. Before you know it, you're even spotting your wife's needs and moods on radar before she has picked them up herself. You learn that both toddler and adult are easier to live with if you can detect and satisfy their desires before they bubble to the surface. In our last conversation, I heard in my mother's voice an end-of-the-line tone, not panicked or suicidal but weary of everything in her wake and within view, on the horizon. I remember the same tone from the time she quit as president of the Jaycee-ettes because the women in the club had organized a boycott of the high school play, *Who's Afraid of Virginia Woolf?*.

My mother was fine. But where had she gone?

Marilyn called and asked me to inspect the contents of my produce drawers.

"What do you need?" I asked.

"Just go look and tell me," she said.

Barefoot and still in my boxer shorts, even though it was dinnertime, I walked across the kitchen to look. I had bean sprouts well past their prime, which had started to yellow like an old man's beard. I had half a jicama, a bag of carrots, one zucchini, three key limes and some flaccid bok choy.

"Bring it all over," she said. "Let's cook. I need diversion. I'm ready to kill my kids."

Marilyn's kitchen is exactly what I envisioned for a caterer. Form follows function, though just a few inches behind. Lots of chrome. No cupboard doors, everything sorted by size and exposed on cherry-wood shelves. Two of the countertops are smooth concrete that subtly decline toward a sink so they can be rinsed off like a platform in a slaughtering house. Yet my favorite fixture is her high-tech German faucet, which emits water in a quiet silky line with no air-bubble texture.

"I've got a *Rugrats* video going downstairs," she told Violet. "Dax and Sarah are already down there."

"Wait a minute," I said. "I don't want her watching *Rugrats.*"

"What's wrong with *Rugrats?*"

"They're poison, Marilyn. The show is one big lesson in how to mock and sneak around authority figures."

"It's not the fucking *Exorcist.*"

"I don't care what your kids do, but I don't want Violet watching it."

"You got any other ideas?"

"You got some glue?" I asked.

"Under the telephone over there."

"And paper?"

"Same place."

I retrieved both then pulled down four boxes of different pastas and dried beans and spread a handful of each on the kitchen table. I squeezed a scalloped, white line out of the Elmer's bottle and placed dried lentils and navy beans onto the glue. "See? An ocean," I said. "You can make pictures."

"Oh, Daddy, let me!"

"I suppose you want me to feel like a bad mom," Marilyn said.

"No."

"Well you have. Thanks. But you haven't been at this as long as I have, you'll get tired of it. The television is your friend, Linc."

"I don't think so."

"Whatever. . . . Here," she said, handing me a glass of chardonnay. "Let's get creative. My favorite part: The initial sparks and engineering."

After sorting through the produce, we decided on a cream-based Mexican curry sauce poured over a mix of mushrooms, zucchini and onions that we grilled outside. Since we had good bread, we decided to forego the pasta and eat like peasants, sopping up the sauce with hunks of a French baguette. For the kids we baked a frozen pizza.

I ate until I hurt, as I'd been doing at almost every meal for weeks now. Punishment or reward, I wasn't sure, but I could not stop, and my stomach was slowly growing into an appendage. In my time at home, food had become a distraction, a time-filler, my principle source of pleasure.

Marilyn took her last bite. "Damn, we're good," she said. "You've got a good feel for food, Linc. You know which ingredients dance well together."

We both sat there in silence, passive from the wine buzz, listening to an Eagles CD playing in the background, the song "Lyin' Eyes," about the woman who drives across town to have an affair.

"You like to dance?" she asked. I nodded.

"Steven and I used to dance before the kids were born."

She then drifted off somewhere, out of the kitchen and into a memory, her eyes set on the Persian rug below as if it were a fire.

I thought about the absence of Jo, not just tonight but in general. Though we had the same goal, the same destination in mind, a well-adjusted, intelligent child, I was beginning to feel as if Jo and I were driving in separate cars on adjacent limited-access freeways: *Look, Violet, there's Mommy! See? Over there. Wave to Mommy. Oh, Mommy's on the car phone, Mommy can't see us.*

Jo has said she wants me to let her in, to include her in more of my and Violet's life at home, but I've grown so accustomed to doing this all without her that it's easier to pretend she's not here. You don't mind a solitary journey as long as you're not expecting anyone.

Suddenly, Dax and Sarah galloped into the kitchen like horses. They wanted Cheetos and Coke, and when Marilyn said no, Dax pulled the step stool from beneath the desk and started reaching for the clear bag of nuclear-orange puffs on top of the refrigerator.

"I said no, Dax! Get down!" She jumped up, ran over and lifted him by the arm off the stool, his legs kicking in midair, his body contorting like a trout that had just been snagged and pulled from the water.

"I hate you Mom! I hate you!" he screamed, trying to kick her. Marilyn dropped him on the floor, returned to the table and took her last drink of wine. Dax followed her, screaming so hard his face looked as red as a baboon's ass. "I hate you! I hate you! I'm gonna tell Dad you ran over his golf shoes!"

Marilyn pushed away from the table, shot up and walked over to the refrigerator. She grabbed the bag of Cheetos and chucked them at him. Dax skipped from the room, his sister close behind.

"Nice kids, huh?" she said, sitting down again.

"I wouldn't have given him the Cheetos," I said.

"Thanks for your opinion, Linc. Just pour me some more wine."

"You said no, you should have stuck with it."

"Give him what he wants and he'll go away. That's what my mother always told me about men. I've learned the same goes for men-in-progress."

"I'm offended."

"Don't be. You're one of us."

"One of who?"

As Carol Merrill used to do in *Let's Make a Deal*, Marilyn motioned with both arms to the kitchen around her, the sink filled with dishes, the bulletin board over the phone covered with its foliage of assorted paper scraps, the errant Cheerios on the floor that Dax and Sarah had been flicking back and forth like hockey pucks.

"One of *us*," she said.

MEXICAN CURRY SAUCE OVER GRILLED VEGETABLES

SERVES FOUR

4 zucchini, julienned into eight strips each
2 large portobello mushrooms
1 handful asparagus spears

1 red bell pepper, sliced thinly

1 large onion, sliced

   Optional: 1 pound shrimp, marinated in 1 cup
orange juice with juice of one lime for 30
minutes. Grill shrimp to desired doneness.

FOR THE CURRY SAUCE:

1 ancho chili, rehydrated and minced

5 cloves garlic, minced

1 tablespoon vegetable oil

1 teaspoon cumin

1 teaspoon oregano

1/8 teaspoon cinnamon

2 tablespoons chicken broth

1 cup half-and-half

1 tablespoon cornstarch dissolved in 2 tablespoons
   water

2–3 tablespoons fresh cilantro, minced

Pour boiling water over the dried chili. Let sit for
30 minutes, then remove stem and seeds. Mince.
The seeds make the pepper spicy, so be sure to get
them all.

   In a grilling basket, grill the zucchini, mushrooms, asparagus, pepper and onions. Set aside.

   Over medium-high heat, brown the minced chili
and garlic in the oil. Add cumin, oregano, cinnamon, then add chicken broth. Reduce heat to
medium. Add half-and-half. Let simmer for ten

minutes, stirring occasionally. Add cornstarch and water. Stir until thickened. Stir in fresh cilantro. Pour over vegetables.

Serve with big hunks of tangy sourdough bread. This is not a mannerly meal; the best part of this recipe is dunking the bread into the sauce.

I'd taken Violet to Memorial Art Gallery to spot shapes in paintings. We'd just returned home, stepping into the dark kitchen with ice cream cones in hand, when I noticed the red light blinking on the answering machine: *Mr. Menner, this is Bob Sloan, the chief engineer with Monroe County. I've left messages with a woman at this number and am still trying to reach you. Please call me at 555-7989.*

"God damn you, Patty!" I yelled. "I'm gonna fire your ass!"

"Daddy is mad," Violet said. "Mad, mad."

The man in charge of the botanical garden project, Sloan had good news and bad. I'd won the bid, yet because of Kodak's recent layoffs in their headquarters downtown the county had put a freeze on all capital construction funds.

"You're not shelving it indefinitely, are you?" I asked. I had worked on publicly financed projects before, and they often get lost forever in limbo-land as public whims evolve and politicians move on.

"No, no," he assured me. "There's a matching foundation grant. We have to follow through or we don't get the money. It's just going to be awhile."

"How long?"

"We're estimating eighteen months."

"A year and a half!"

"I'm afraid so. No sooner than that anyway."

I hung up and dropped into a kitchen chair at the table, feeling as limp and empty and salvageable as room-temperature, raw chicken skin. I'd made the mistake of investing too much hope in that single project. In my mind, for months, as I washed dishes and vacuumed and wiped the poop from Violet's butt, I'd been arranging and rearranging succulents and designing an underground irrigation system. This project was going to be my launch. I wouldn't have to go out and forage for contracts like mushrooms in a dark, unfamiliar forest. The desert ecosystem was going to throw open the door. Hey, everyone, here he is! The California Golden Boy has arrived! Stand in line!

I'm more of an artist and gardener than a salesman. I do not like being in a position of need, and with no high-profile, vanity job this is exactly where I was. I wondered whether I should wait eighteen months for a project that might never transpire.

From my chair at the table, I looked out into the dining room. My passion flower vine had continued to grow at grass speed, blindly reaching in all directions to find something to climb on. For days, it slowly bent this way and that, until one afternoon it had grown long enough to bump into the low-hanging chandelier over the dining-room table. Within hours, the tendril made two loops around the crystal arm, anchoring the plant to the light.

The plant continued to meander in and out of the chandelier until it grew bored then continued on up the stem of the light to the ceiling. Jo wanted to cut it off, but I threatened her life. I could not penalize something so blind but undaunted, an exotic thriving in unnatural surroundings.

Jo and I had hosted a United Way fund-raising party at the house, so word of my plants had spread, and I started getting calls from women around Pittsford: "Ginny Martin told me you're good with plants, and I have this one with yellow leaves . . ."

Most housewives kill plants, they drown them, and it's easy to see why. Housewives spend their days filling voids. Stomachs and cookie jars and dry potted plants, sugar bowls and egos and bathtubs and soap dispensers and refrigerators and juice glasses and pillowcases and washing machines and cat boxes and toilet-paper holders. We subconsciously think that if we fill everything to the very top we'll have more time before it needs to be filled again. Clean your plate. One more sip. Just another inch of water.

I tell the women who call that the common house plant is one thing they should neglect, and the more they ignore it the more it will flourish. But still they water because water is good and clean and everything likes water, and as the leaves continue to yellow and drop to the carpeting they pour on more and more and more until it drowns and dies and is set out with the garbage on Wednesday night.

I had to get Violet toilet trained or she couldn't go to the Montessori preschool I'd set my sights on. I knew she could do it; she'd memorized *Once Upon a Potty*, both the book and video. I quizzed her over breakfast and lunch. I'd ask her things like, "Okay, what do you do when you pull down your underwear?"

"Sit on potty," she says.

"Good. Then what?"

"Go tee-tee."

"Okay, then what?"

"Flush."

"No, no, no, wipe pee-pee then flush."

"Okay. Wipe pee-pee. Flush."

Still, we had only about a 25 percent success rate, thanks mainly to my prompting her to go whenever I saw her touching her crotch and getting jumpy, doing what I call the potty polka.

I was immersed in a task, replacing the washers in the kitchen faucet, when I noticed that Violet had been playing in her room a little too long. She normally would float in and out like a bee pollinating flowers, but it had been at least thirty minutes since I'd heard or seen any trace of her.

I peeked in her door and was hit by the sweet, meaty stench of fresh shit, warmed from the late-afternoon sun pouring through her window. Not only had Violet pooped in her underwear, she'd scooped it out like mud and tried to hide it—in the toy box, in her drawers, under the bed, in the closet. Then she wiped her hands on the fabric-covered blinds, the walls, the mattress, the carpet.

"Violet!"

"Oh, Daddy! Oh, oh, oh, oh!"

She turned away from the toy box, her hands covered with so much shit it looked as if she'd been playing in chocolate cake batter.

"You're damn right 'oh, oh, oh'! I'm furious, girl!"

"Oh, Daddy! It's a big mess!"

"You know better than this, Violet. I'm so pissed! You don't know how pissed I am. I am so goddamned pissed!"

"My daddy is so pissed," she said, nodding her head with a scowl, *my* scowl, knowing it was best to match the mood, not try and change it.

I instinctively reached for the phone and called Jo, yanking her out of a meeting.

"You will not fucking believe what's just happened."

"Oh, my God, Lincoln. What? Is it Violet? Is she okay?"

"There is shit all over the bedroom, Jo. It's on the duvet cover, it's on the blinds. Goddamnit, it's even smeared into the grain of the maple. I'll never get it all out!"

"Calm down, Lincoln."

"I am so sick of this shit I can't stand it any longer!"

"Lincoln . . ."

"But it looks like a goddamned sewer exploded! There is no way this room will ever smell the same."

"What do you want me to do?"

"Nothing! There's nothing you can do!"

"I'm sorry, honey, but then why did you call?"

"Because it's your job to listen to me bitch about this, okay? I'm shielding you from all this potty-training crap, the least you can do is listen!"

I looked down at Violet, who stood beside me, her eyes wide with fear. She'd never seen me this mad. There was a horizontal smudge of poop under her nose from where she had tried to wipe away a runny booger.

"Okay, okay, Jo, I'm sorry I bothered you. I've got it under control."

"You sure?"

"I'm sure. Bye. Sorry."

"Come on!" I said to Violet. "And don't touch anything. Your hands are a mess."

"Yes, my hands are a mess."

We went down to the kitchen and retrieved rags, paper towels, a spatula, trash bags and a bucket of warm water with Lysol. I knew it would be easier and faster for me to clean it all, but that wouldn't get the point across.

"Okay, start cleaning it up," I said, using the spatula to scoop up a thick brown smudge from the comforter on her bed. "Like this."

"Oh, Daddy, no."

"Oh, Daddy, yes! Now get going."

With the wet rags I followed her from spot to spot, cleaning for more than an hour, my knuckles bleeding from carpet burns. Some spots I had to scrub six or seven times, and even then there remained a ghost of a stain. We carted all her toys to the bathtub and washed them in

Clorox. We laundered all the bedding and clothes, seven loads worth. We swabbed down the walls and maple furniture with Lysol. We set up fans and opened the windows to dry out the scene of the crime.

Finally, we bathed and sat down for a late lunch of peas, tortellini and prosciutto tossed with toasted walnut oil and salt. Though exhausting, the cleaning proved to be cathartic, and I calmed down enough to recognize that I was proud of my daughter's thoroughness.

"You did a good job helping me, Violet. It was a big mess and you never complained."

"Big poopy mess," she said.

"Humongous poopy mess. Enough poop to fill a lake."

"A ocean!"

"How did all of that come from one little girl?"

"Oh, Daddy! Poopy is made from food. You told me."

I walked over, scooped her into my arms and smothered her neck in kisses, Violet breaking into a string of giggles that reminded me of falling dominoes.

"I know a poem about the ocean," I said. "I saw it in the book Grandma Jean sent you. Go find it, and let's cuddle and read."

I set my lips and eyes on autopilot as I read *Whales in the Harbor* by Nimoi Kiatu, the story of a mommy orca who loses then finds her babies. I can read to Violet and drift away on journeys of my own, and this time I pictured myself flying, arms out to my side like Christ on the cross, traversing the volatile landscape of my emotions that day, the misty forest of early morning, sudden, jagged peaks of midday turning into plains that sloped down to ocean, and in the distance, land, and I knew it soon would start all over again. How could my entire life—my work and play, joy and unhappiness, satisfaction and frustration, freedom and captivity—all come from this little creature on my lap, who I love, more at this moment, less at others?

Which reminded me: *Lessen tension on coil rod of garage door.*

Which reminded me: *Change car-insurance deductible.*

Which reminded me: *Violet's car seat.*

What was New York's age limit for child restraints?

Restrain.

Refrain.

Please refrain from smoking. Smoking is not permitted in the lavatories.

Would I ever get a vacation away from my daughter?

Fast-and-Easy Tortellini with Peas and Prosciutto

SERVES FOUR

2 containers fresh tortellini pasta from the
   refrigerated grocery case (These usually are
   somewhere near the bacon and hot dogs.)
1 cup frozen peas
1 cup prosciutto, cut into strips

2 tablespoons toasted walnut oil
  Kosher or sea salt and pepper

Cook pasta according to instructions on packet.
When finished, stir in all ingredients. The peas will
defrost soon after contact with the hot pasta. Salt
and pepper to taste. You'll be surprised how many
kids love this easy meal.

"Daddy, look!" Violet exclaimed, taking the crinkly white sack from Patty. "She's giving me a present!"

"It's from Rosa's Dollar Store," Patty said, taking off her shiny purple parka.

"Can I open it now?"

"Yeah, yeah, open it already," she said.

From the sack Violet pulled a boxed Barbie dressed in a hot-pink bikini, smiling at us through clear plastic.

"Oh, Patty! I love this. I looooove this!"

"Malibu Beach Barbie," I said.

"It was that or Cool Shopping Barbie, but with you being from California and all I thought you'd like this."

"Daddy, look at her tiny little sunglasses!"

"Yes, sweetheart, I see. . . . Patty?"

"Yeah?"

We started walking back to the kitchen, leaving Violet with her Barbie in the living room.

"You've noticed that Violet doesn't have a single Barbie—right?"

" 'Course I did! Every little girl needs a Barbie."

"Did it ever dawn on you that it might be intentional?"

Though I'd already washed the lunch dishes, Patty

proceeded to rinse the sink with the vegetable sprayer, ridding it of any demons I might have missed.

"Why do you do that?" I asked.

"What?"

"You always rinse out the sink, even when it doesn't need it. Why?"

"No I don't."

"Yes, you do."

"Well, I don't know. You can't get things too clean."

"I don't like Barbies," I said.

"What do you mean you don't like Barbies?"

"I think they send some sick messages to little girls."

"What? There's nothin' wrong with Barbies. You're crazy."

"Barbies teach the girls of our culture an unrealistic version of beauty."

"Whadaya mean?"

"Look at those breasts and waist, Patty."

"Look at 'em, all right! Makes me wish I was young."

"They're not realistic, no one with hooters like that can stand that straight. And we're teaching little girls that this is the standard of beauty in this culture, and they're never going to be happy with themselves. This is why our society has such a huge problem with bulimia."

"What do you mean bulimia, what's that?"

A prime candidate, I thought. Don't go there.

"And I think Barbie condones wearing makeup," I said. "And I don't like that, either. She's the Antichrist of the natural state."

Patty stopped wiping out the sink and looked up at me with that disgusted "duhhh!" look of a teenager who's just been told her skirt is too short for school, head cocked, nose scrunched, teeth slightly bared like a growling tiger, the antiauthority scowl of television sitcoms, broadcast to a world void of individual creativity and hungry for behavioral templates. Violet would not know such a look.

"You're crazy," she said. "What's wrong with a little makeup?"

"I don't take my job lightly, Patty. I'm responsible for the development of my daughter."

"Well you gotta relax about it. She's just a kid."

"And you've got to get better at taking phone messages."

Which reminded me: *Re-record voice mail message.*

Call Marilyn about kids' trip to zoo.

Why doesn't Marilyn ever smile?

Do I smile anymore?

Swollen gums.

Find dentist.

Moist mouth.

Say ahhhh . . .

Dark pinkness of inner flesh.

Need to get laid.

No energy.

Call Rochester Electric for free energy audit.

I plucked my car keys from the hook on the wall beside the telephone. "I'm going to Barnes & Noble," I said. "Make sure you and Violet take a walk this morning."

I was scanning the home-and-garden magazine section, a steaming espresso in hand, when the cover of *Garden Design* jumped out at me like the photo of an old girlfriend. It was the DiPasso yard in Laguna Hills, which I'd designed two years earlier.

Problem. Big problem. The story was about Jean Claude Simosy, an alleged L.A. landscape architect who considered me a peer but in reality was a hack. In the story, he'd actually added a few plants and claimed the garden as his own creation, rambling on and on about this line and that curve, and they were my lines, my curves, and this jerk had no idea what he was talking about.

I tried to call Jean Claude on my cell phone. His secretary—secretary!—answered and said he was too busy.

"He's not accepting new clients," she said.

"I'm not a client," I replied. "I'm a mad landscaper who's gonna sue his ass!"

I hung up, realizing the call was fruitless and nothing more than a jab in the dark. There was a bigger issue here: I was fading like a Rochester pansy in June, and I would soon disappear, and all those years of building a reputation would be wasted. I felt as helpless as Amelia Earhart, alive on some island, reading a copy of *Aviation Today* that had washed up on the beach.

That night, after getting Violet to bed, I went down to the basement and sought out the Rubbermaid plastic tub filled with the magazine and newspaper clippings of my career. I sat down on the floor in the middle of the living room with a six-pack of Bass Ale and began to read through them all.

Jo woke me at one A.M. I'd fallen asleep—passed out?—on the floor.

"Okay, tell me I'm pathetic," I said, sitting up on the carpet.

"Oh, Lincoln." She touched my forehead. "You have no idea how guilty this makes me feel."

"I make my own choices, Jo. I'm responsible for me, you're not."

She set down her black leather briefcase and sat next to me on the floor, like a parent dropping down to the height of a child in hopes of closing, or narrowing, some communication gap.

"The desert job was just one gig, Lincoln."

"That's not it," I said.

"What then?"

"I'm just so tired of feeling bad about myself. I'm not doing anything constructive. I'm just floating out there, and no one knows I'm alive. No one except Violet."

Jo rested her hands on my cheeks, guided my head and gaze upward and looked in my eyes. "Then run an ad in the *Democrat and Chronicle* and find some work."

"But you need me at home right now," I said. "You're never here. What would happen to Violet if I wasn't home? Our lives would be chaos."

"That's why we have Patty," she said.

"She can't do a good job."

"This sounds like a control issue, Linc."

But it was more than that, I knew it now. I had not worked outside the house for more than three months, and the more time that passed, the less confidence I had in my abilities to flourish outside this controlled environment that I myself had created and perpetuated. The tiny creek separating my former successful business and a new business had widened into a canyon, and the chasm grew more each day. A control issue? Perhaps, but not completely. I liked the idea of being the life-support system, essential as oxygen, for two other humans.

"Maybe I'm just tired of landscaping," I said. "Maybe I should try something different."

"Okay . . ."

"Maybe catering . . . Marilyn and I were talking about it."

"I don't like that idea."

"I wish you'd relax about her, Jo."

"I can't, Lincoln. I'm grateful she's your friend, you need friends. But I don't like how you two drink wine all day long and sit out in the wading pool with the kids. And I'm sure her husband feels the same way I do."

"You're overreacting."

"You're a man at home, Lincoln. You cook and clean and you're excellent with children. That's very sexy. You've got to navigate this friendship carefully. This journey might be taking you somewhere you don't want to go."

"How do you know?"

She sighed and stood up from the floor. "I don't know for sure."

"You've never met her," I said.

"I've seen her in the yard, Lincoln. She's your type. Don't deny it."

"You mean her boobs."

"Bingo."

Marilyn most definitely was not unattractive. Indeed, I might have messed around with her in a different situation. Yet I did not need sex, I needed companionship. My desire for adult conversation was so strong it extinguished any embers of sexual attraction I might have had, and Marilyn, other than Jo, was my only outlet for this. There had been occasional, awkward moments of silence, when Marilyn would look at me, awaiting a response to a safely oblique and indirect sexual prompt she had just delivered, and I would play dumb and let it roll over me like a wave, crashing then dying on the sand. I can get away with this because I'm a man, and women know that men, *most* men, cannot grasp nuance or subtlety.

"I just get paranoid because she's beautiful," Jo said. "And she's here, and I'm not, and we don't have intimate moments anymore. When was the last time we made love? A month ago? . . . Is something wrong with us, Lincoln? Is there something wrong with me?"

That previous week, while cleaning the master bathroom, I had found copies of *Marie Claire* and *Cosmopolitan*, reading materials I'd never seen in our home. The latter had a teaser on the front page that asked, "Working Women: Is Your Libido on Ice? Take Our Test." I sat down on the john, plucked a pen from my back pocket and opened to page one hundred seventy. Jo, however, had already filled in the blanks. Guilt be damned, I began to read.

Maybe it's his problem, not yours: Is he a nice guy? Is he someone you WANT to sleep with?

A check mark in the *yes* box, thank God.

How often do you think about having sex?

Twice a month, she marked.

How often does your partner think about sex?

There was only a question mark.

Thank God. At least it wasn't just me who was dead down there. Aggressive as she is, Jo historically has waited on me to initiate our lovemaking, and I'd been taking no initiative. Perhaps I'd learned these past few months that men seek sex more often because they have more leisure time. When a woman—and that's obviously me in this case—has a moment of leisure, when everyone and everything is inexplicably, temporarily, magically satisfied, she grabs it for herself and hides until someone with a need discovers her. I wanted sex, but Jo wasn't home when I had the time and the inclination. I had settled for the low-impact, low-energy alternative of masturbation. It was easier, faster, it took care of a need without reliance upon anyone. Still, I worried if she was still attracted to me, if she could desire a man with a toggle switch in his brain that flips his personality back and forth between man and woman: *Hey, baby, time to worship the tower of power. . . . Oh, honey, let Daddy kiss your boo-boo.*

"Lincoln, answer me," she said. "Please."

"No, Jo. There's nothing wrong with you."

"Then what? Tell me there's nothing going on with Marilyn."

"I can't believe you! Why are you being so paranoid?"

"I'm being insecure, not paranoid," she said.

"You don't trust me, do you? Evidently you've forgotten how strong I am."

"I wonder about your strength nowadays, Lincoln. It seems to have diminished."

Not diminished, I thought, just under renovation. Coming soon to a circus freak show near you: *The Strong Man Who Understands Women.*

Jo and I lay on the couch, watching a brainless Charles Grodin movie on one of those rare Friday evenings she was not working.

The phone rang. "I'm not here," she said.

It was Marilyn, panicked. Sixteen people, the board of Wildwood Country Club and their spouses, were due for dinner in one hour, and the meal was not falling into place as she'd planned because she'd been drinking all afternoon. The roast, burned. The dough for the rolls, flat.

"And I don't have a vegetable," she said.

"I'll be right over."

As I dug through the vegetable bin, Jo stood behind me, talking. "I can't believe you're leaving on my only night at home."

"This is called nurturing a friendship," I said.

"Lincoln, this is the only night I've been home for more than a week."

"Marilyn has been good to me, she's included me, and that's more than I can say for the rest of the bitches in Pittsford."

"I don't think this bodes well for our relationship."

"And I think you're overreacting. She needs my help, Jo."

I leaned down and kissed her forehead. "Do me a favor. When the buzzer goes off, take the chickens out of the convection oven and call me." And I hurried away with a crinkly grocery sack of vegetables and herbs.

Marilyn was far enough gone that she abandoned the meal to me the second I burst through the back door. She just stood to the side and watched, as if I were a paramedic who had come to save the victim she'd been trying to resuscitate on the street. I would ask for a cooking utensil or bowl and Marilyn would hurriedly retrieve it, hand it over, then return again to the wings and watch as I tried to whip and cut and sauté life into this dying meal. From the corner of my eye I noticed her standing in the corner of the room, hugging her elbows and trembling like some junkie coming down from an awful trip. Obviously I'd underestimated her fear of Steven.

Eventually, she trailed off to shower and dress. I was cutting zucchini and summer squash when Steven walked in from the garage. Though I'd seen him from afar we had never actually met. I avoided Marilyn's house while he was in town, thinking he'd want time alone with his family.

"Who the hell are you?" he asked.

"The cook," I said.

"A caterer?"

"Sure."

"It's only sixteen people. What the hell is she hiring a caterer for? Where is she?"

"I think she's getting dressed."

The doorbell rang. Seconds later I heard Marilyn's voice explode in a boisterous, happy greeting. She stalled them with cocktails for a good half hour, which gave me enough time to make a sauce and whisk together a respectable dressing.

Finally, everyone seated, Marilyn walked into the kitchen. She wore a short black dress and silver Mexican earrings that looked like road-runner feet. And on her own feet, leather step-in shoes with bare legs, despite the cold November evening.

"It smells fantastic!" she said. And it did. From scratch, I'd made a complete meal in forty-five minutes. A baked Italian entrée of chicken and turnips in a cream sauce of curry and currants. Tossed salad with a homemade Dijon dressing. Two loaves of good French bread I'd frozen the week before. Tomatoes baked with olives and rosemary and a hint of anchovy.

Platter by platter, Marilyn served the food while I hid in the kitchen.

"What is this, Marilyn?" I heard Steven ask.

"It's northern Italian, of course," she said.

"What happened to the roast?" he asked.

Then, another voice I hadn't yet heard, a man's: "This is delicious, Marilyn, better than roast."

"Thank you."

And a woman: "I want the recipe for this, Marilyn. What did you do to these tomatoes?" It was the last comment I heard before I gathered up my spices and sneaked out the back door.

I slept in the next morning, waking up at about ten. Jo had fed Violet and taken her out somewhere. She'd set on the kitchen table a note that evidently had been taped to the front door: *Thanks Superman. I owe you a dinner. M.*

Next to the note was a folded section of the classifieds with a help-wanted ad circled in orange crayon. Robins and Fischer, upstate New York's largest nursery, was looking for someone to head their commercial landscape accounts.

Jo had marked in her fountain pen, *It's meant to be. No one has more credentials for this than you. Call them for an interview, but only if you want to. I love you, and thanks for everything you do for us.*

It did look promising. I sat down at my kitchen desk, paid a few bills then finally summoned up the nerve to call and set up an appointment for Monday. I was standing up from my desk when I heard the ping of my e-mail. I signed

in and, to my great surprise, found a letter from my
mother.

> *Date: Sat. 14 Nov.*
> *From: SavannahLibsys@fgi.gov*
> *To: LincolnM@aol.com*
> *Lincoln: this is your mother. Nooooooo, I have not gone*
> *off the deep end . . . the car was the final straw. . . . . .*
> *your father told me he'd sold it and he wanted me to*
> *take it into the dealership for a cleaning. . . . . . but*
> *starting smoking was another reason for leaving. . . . . .*
> *How can a man who has lived with you for thirty-four*
> *years decide to pursue a vice that leaves his wife wheez-*
> *ing for air? I smoke outside, he says. It's the smell, Don,*
> *I tell him, not the smoke, I'm allergic to the smell. Oh, I*
> *didn't know that, he says, though he's heard it two*
> *thousand times. . . . and then he does it again and*
> *sprays himself with Lysol and is so insensitive he*
> *doesn't even know that I know.*
> *. . . . . . I don't know why I left; I just didn't want to*
> *give up the car and I didn't feel like fighting. You know*
> *it's impossible to fight your father the glacier. I told him*
> *I was going to drive it for a final farewell over to Long*
> *John Silver's on Saguaro Boulevard, and that's really*
> *all I was going to do, but I went through the drive-*
> *through and I just kept on driving. . . . . I have every-*
> *thing I need in my wonderful, big car. Your father would*
> *die—I'm eating potato chips in it, I'm even driving on*
> *dirt roads. . . . . I stayed in a Hyatt last night and*

*ordered a dirty movie. . . . . I sketched one of the his-
toric churches in town—an exquisite Romanesque—
that I plan on painting somewhere down the road . . .
also saw Lady Chablis (you know, the female imperson-
ator from Midnight in the Garden of Good and Evil)
sing at a club. I looked really hard for his/her candy but
he/she hides it well. Do not tell your father you heard
from me, I want him to sweat. Kiss Violet and
Josephine."*

Jo and I called this car the Mayflower, a huge French-blue
lug of a rectangle. My mother had claimed it had saved her
life. Earlier this year she got caught in a hellacious storm
up near Placerville, the biggest snow in sixteen years, so
she settled in for hibernation. She coated her entire body in
Vaseline then dressed in layers. She had battery-operated
hot curlers that she heated up and stuck in her shoes and
under her arms. She also had her Itty Bitty Booklight, so
fifteen hours later when a state trooper would spot a pair of
women's red panties peeking through a drift, tied to the radio antenna of a big Lincoln, he would be surprised to find
beneath the snow a calm woman who not only appeared to
be warm and safe but also sufficiently entertained.

Mom had bonded with this car, which is something
you shouldn't do if you're a car dealer's wife. It's like a
cattleman's daughter bonding with a calf: Get too close
and you'll break your heart.

I decided not to tell Jo about this, at least not yet. I
decided to grant Mom her secrecy, which surprised me

because I generally share everything with Jo. My mother had escaped what she considered an unhappy, empty world and for the first time in memory seemed to have my father's attention. Still, I wondered whether my reluctance to reveal her secret was born out of caregiver solidarity or a need for vicarious living.

LINC'S BAKED TOMATOES

SERVES FOUR

 4 large tomatoes
 2 cloves garlic, minced
 $1/8$ teaspoon fresh rosemary
 $1/2$ of 1 anchovy filet (You can always store the
     remaining filets in a Tupperware container with
     olive oil.)
 8 kalamata olives
    Pinch of salt
 2 teaspoons olive oil
    Fresh ground pepper

Preheat oven to 350°. Grind the garlic, rosemary, anchovy and olives together using a mortar and pestle, and adding the salt to help break it up. (Kosher salt works better at this than normal, finer table salt.) Add the olive oil and mix it into this paste. Cut the tomatoes in half, then spread a bit of this mixture onto the exposed flat side of each tomato. Pepper each tomato, then set into a baking dish, flat side up, and bake for one hour. If you're in a hurry, turn the heat up to 400° and subtract fifteen minutes. This can be served with leftover chicken or some good bread and cheese. A very easy meal, and everyone will think you've gone to lots of trouble.

It had snowed ten inches during the night. After breakfast, Violet and I dressed in our coats, mittens and hats and went outside to climb what Jo and I have named Mount Menner. Instead of carrying all that snow to another location, the Pittsford road crews scoop it up and dump it in the middle of the Quail Run cul-de-sac. Since the winter temperatures rarely stretch above freezing, the white mountain grows and grows like a pile of dirty laundry. I've heard that by March it reaches skyward for more than twenty feet, and the last of that snow will not disappear until the first week in June.

I'd called Dax and Sarah to tell them we were going out. They always come. Other kids trickle out as well, drawn by the growls and melodramatic squeals of make-believe fear. I am the Pied Piper when I stand atop Mount Menner. To the children who don't know me, I am "crazy monster man."

They climbed again and again, trying to dislodge me from the summit. I growled and roared, picking them up, holding them aloft like King Kong then pushing them down the glacier on their bellies or backs. Violet and the other meek children ran around at the bottom of the mountain, screaming, "What can we do? Help us! The monster! Oh!"

One boy, maybe about twelve, reached the summit and grabbed for my legs. He was too big to play, he'd hurt either me or one of the other kids. There's just too much body mass and anger and testosterone in boys that age. This kind of thing happens all the time at the McDonald's Playland in Perinton. I frequently have to approach mothers and ask them to purge their sons from Playland. I'll say, "You see, they're taller than the Hamburgler height guide. This is reserved for small children for their safety. Your children are taller than Hamburgler, and that means they shouldn't be inside Playland. As mothers, I'm sure you won't mind." But they do, and they glare because instead of diving back into blissful girly chit-chat with their friends they now have to watch their kids as they should have been doing in the first place.

"Whoa, son," I said to the boy on Mount Menner. "You're too big to play. You're gonna hurt me. This is for the little kids."

He grabbed and rocked my legs, trying to topple me over.

"I said, Stop!"

"Oh yeah? Who's gonna make me, weirdo?" he said.

I reached down, pried off his fingers and picked the little son-of-a-bitch up by the chest of his snow suit, lifting him until our noses touched.

"I. Asked. You. To. Stop! Stop means stop. You will listen to me because I am an adult." I dropped him into the snow, and he ran down the cul-de-sac, back home.

Ten minutes later, his mother appeared in her Burberry trench coat and duck boots, the official leisure footwear of Pittsford. Fashion in this affluent suburb is uptight, to say the least. The men shave on the weekends and tuck in their T-shirts. Colors that fall outside the safe earth-tone spectrum are reserved exclusively for clothes worn during winter vacation in Fort Myers.

"Excuse me!" she yelled from the bottom of Mount Menner.

"Yeeeeeessss," I replied, prying Dax's fingers from my ankle.

"My son says you hurt him."

I yelled back down, "Does he look hurt to you?"

"You're awfully rough with these children."

"They are having an awful time, aren't they?"

I told Dax and the others to chill for a minute, and I tromped down Mount Menner to meet her at the bottom.

"Listen, your son is too big to play this game," I said, brusquely wiping the snow from my shoulders. "One of these smaller kids is gonna get hurt. I'm trying to be responsible here. I asked your son to stop. He didn't stop. He's pissed because someone told him what to do. I guess that doesn't happen very often."

She exhaled forcefully, like a horse in the cold air, looking for words, a comeback, but what could she say?

"Do you know who my husband is?" she asked.

Stay-at-homers often stand beneath the identity umbrella of their husbands. It is because they feel invisible.

"That answer would be no, I do not know your husband."

"My husband is president and general manager of TransAmerica Cablevision."

The sentence ended with intonation slightly curving upward. Obviously I was supposed to respond.

"Gosh," I said. "Then I probably shouldn't tell you that we don't subscribe to cable."

"My husband's going to call you."

"I can't wait to meet him. My name's Linc Menner, this is Mount Menner," I said, pointing to the snow pile. "I'm the new child molester who's moved into the neighborhood."

Malibu Beach Barbie soon proved to be as evil as I'd feared. Violet was obsessed with her for all the wrong reasons, always combing the hair and changing her in and out of the only two outfits she had, the pink bikini and a glittery teal plastic jumpsuit.

"Oh, Daddy, just look at her." Violet had propped Barbie up against the Cheerios box as she ate breakfast. "She's the most beautiful lady in the whole world. I want to be Barbie."

"Just what do you like about her?" I asked.

"I like Barbie's shoes. . . . And she's soooooo pretty."

"But what do you mean by pretty?"

"Daddy, you know what pretty is. Bootiful."

"But beautiful on the outside doesn't mean beautiful on the inside."

I scanned the living room for a small toy and found a little green-and-white stuffed doggy, about the size of a muffin, that Violet had found abandoned in a seat in the Tilt-a-Whirl at Sea Breeze.

"Okay, watch this," I said, picking up the Barbie. "Here comes little doggy walking down the street. Barbie sees him and yells, 'Oh! I hate dogs! Their hair messes up my beautiful clothes! Get out of here, you stupid mutt!' And she kicks him . . . like this . . . and gives him a karate chop . . . like that!"

"Daddy! You're hurting the doggy."

"No, no, honey, Barbie is hurting the doggy."

"Barbies don't hurt doggies."

"No, Barbies *look* sweet and kind, but sometimes the prettiest people are the meanest and dumbest. And you know why? Because they're so worried about what they look like that they don't even stop to think of anyone else."

Violet paused, looking reflective, almost frowning as she chewed her cereal, as if I'd snatched something special from her grip.

"But this Barbie is going to college," she finally said.

"If she can get into college. Do you think this Barbie's smart enough?"

"Yes."

"Good. Because being pretty doesn't get you into

college, and it doesn't make you any money. And being pretty doesn't mean you're smart or nice."

"Mommy's pretty and smart."

"Yes, she is, honey, you're right. But very few women are like that."

"Mommy has big boobies like Barbie."

I couldn't help but laugh. I love those little Tourette's-like comments that sputter from the mouths of children like unexpected farts.

I walked over to the counter to sort through the mail. I have an excellent system for mail sorting. Clothing catalogs go in one basket, house-related catalogs in another. I also have my Jo basket, in which I put anything that I think she needs to see, including personal mail, opened with envelopes discarded.

I opened to the phone bill and got a huge surprise—forty-six collect phone calls from the Monroe County Jail.

Immediately I called Patty. This could not wait until tomorrow.

"What the hell are all these collect calls doing on the phone bill?" I asked.

"Oh, those. I was gonna tell ya about those."

"Who do you know in the Monroe County Jail?"

"That's Bobby."

"Bobby?"

"My boyfriend."

"Your boyfriend's in prison?"

"Not prison, just jail. And only because his ex-wife ratted on him. Two friggin' tires from Anatelli's is all he took, and they sent him to jail. They just leave those things out in front of the store, What do they expect?"

"There must be eighty dollars of calls here."

"Eighty bucks! Yeesh! I don't have eighty bucks."

"Then I'll have to take it out of your pay."

"At least I only have him call when you're gone."

"Sometimes he calls four times in an hour, Patty."

"He misses me," she said. "He's a real momma's boy. He misses my spaetzle."

Marilyn called and asked me to jump her Suburban. The battery had died because Dax had left the reading light on in the back seat. "We might as well go to the mall when we're done," she said. "I've got to get out of the house before I go crazy."

With the kids setting the course, we first hit the Disney Store, which was all right with me because I wanted to buy Violet some underwear as positive reinforcement. She was still wetting in her pants and stashing the soiled clothes behind the bed or beneath the sofa. This could not go on forever. Or could it?

I approached one of the young clerks in the blue varsity cardigans.

"Where's your underwear with little Snow Whites on them?" I asked.

She looked at me, confused. "We don't have underwear with Snow White."

"Yes you do, I've seen them. My friend's daughter has some."

The clerk, a young woman, looked at Marilyn and shared that smug, he-doesn't-get-it, female-solidarity smile that pisses me off so much because it excludes me from a world that I rightly belong to and understand.

"You mean *panties*," she corrected.

"Okay then: panties."

We decided to eat lunch at Ruby Tuesday because they had a full bar and good macaroni and cheese and chicken fingers for the kids.

"Let's order some wine."

"You're driving, Marilyn."

"Not anymore," she replied, tossing the keys to me over the table.

The waiter appeared with chicken finger baskets for the kids, who miraculously had been quietly entertained with coloring the tropical scenes on their paper placemats.

"Don't look now," Marilyn said, "but Carolyn Zentis is at five o'clock, over by the big stop sign on the wall."

"Zentis?"

"Your friend from the snow mountain. Mrs. Burberry."

"How did you know about our tiff in the snow?"

"They all talk about you, Linc. Get real. Surely you know that."

"You're kidding me."

"Sexy man moves into the neighborhood as a mom? Don't you think it's just too much of a spicy tidbit for our boring lives?"

"Come on."

"Men are not part of the upscale suburban landscape, Linc. You've learned that by now. Don't act so naïve."

I wasn't listening, at least not fully. The word that sent my mind racing had been uttered ten seconds earlier: sexy. I'm convinced that having a baby in tow extinguishes one's sexuality. I remember reacting differently to good-looking women who carried or pushed babies in strollers, and now I know why. Because of time famine, because of priority changes and a quantum shift in focus, once you're a primary caregiver the sexual side of your persona gets shoved into a dark closet, and any flirtation catches you off guard. Over the past several months, the demands of motherhood slowly, cumulatively, like piling quilts on top of each other, had begun to smother my sexual identity. Child care requires such intense focus on points away from you. You look outward and forward, left and right, but the last place you ever seem to look is down there, at yourself. You mean you find me attractive? *Sexually* attractive?

I recalled the week before, my encounter with the new neighbors. A new family had moved into one of the homes across the street, and since two neighbors had welcomed us to the neighborhood with cookies and wine, I thought it was my duty to pass on the torch of hospitality with a loaf of five-grain sourdough bread.

The woman who answered the door looked at me with that forced look of politeness employed by clerks at upscale women's clothing stores, the pushed smile, chin up, the nose ever so slightly raised in the air, as if they're sniffing you out. I was wearing blue jeans, a flannel shirt and two days' beard, and she most likely thought I was some farmer from the Finger Lakes region trying to sell his firewood or snow-plowing services.

"Can I help you?" she asked.

"I'm Linc Menner from sixteen-forty-two," I said, pointing across the street. "Here." I held out the loaf of bread. "I made this myself. Welcome to the neighborhood."

She looked at the bread, then again at me, her eyes and brows showing puzzlement, the meaningless smile refusing to collapse. Something obviously did not seem right to her. This woman would not take the bread from my hands.

"Uh . . . you live across the street?" she asked.

"Yes. Right there. We're new, too, been here just over four months. . . . I noticed you have a daughter."

"Yes . . ."

"And she's how old?"

"Uh . . . Four."

"My daughter's three. We just finished potty training, well not actually finished, but I think the worst is over."

"Uh-huh . . ."

"Is your daughter potty trained?"

"Excuse me . . . Could you wait a minute, please? You probably want to talk to my husband."

She looked over her shoulder and yelled, "John! Can you come here?"

I realized then I should have brought Violet along. Women are more comfortable around me if I have Violet

in tow, as if she were a chaperone or accessory that emasculated me in some way. A baby for a man is a softening
agent, like Downy in the rinse cycle. Often, when I cross
the street looking like I usually do—two or three days of
beard stubble, khaki pants, sandals with socks—I hear the
electric click of doors being locked as I approach the cars.
My size does not help any; I'm six three, two hundred and
thirty, a size forty-eight dinner jacket. Still, I rarely get this
reaction if I'm carrying Violet in my arms, no matter how
grungy I look.

Husband John, obviously home helping with the move,
came to his frightened wife's rescue. I did the benign, guy
chit-chat thing for a minute or two then left. With the
bread.

This woman's reaction, not unusual, reminded me of
that admonition we all were raised with: "Don't take candy
from strangers." What they meant, of course, was candy
from men, and grown women are still wary any time a man
offers them something. Women are the givers, men are the
takers, and derivations from that rule are suspect. Last
month, with Violet in my arm, I tried to give away an extra
50-percent-off coupon at the grand opening of Steinmart,
though no one would accept it. I intentionally dropped it
on the floor on the way out, giving it safe, neutral status.
Someone snatched it up within ten seconds.

Marilyn drank the last finger of wine and motioned to
the waiter for another.

"Come on and have some wine," she said.

"Can't," I replied, "I'm the driver."

"Suit yourself."

"Daddy, daddy, ketchup please, ketchup please." I reached for the new bottle and unscrewed the white top, then poured a puddle near the rim of Violet's plate.

"Me, too," Dax said, his mouth full of fries.

"Excuse me?" I replied. "Me, too what?"

"Me too ketchup."

"How about, 'May I have some ketchup, please?' "

"Please," he said.

"Good. Thank you," I said, handing him the bottle.

I returned my focus to Marilyn. "But why do they all seem to hate me?"

"Hate you?"

"They don't even wave from the safety of their cars."

"They'd wave if you weren't good-looking. They'd wave if you were hugely fat and bald and ugly."

"That's not fair."

"And these women don't like their husbands, some of them do but not all of them. You're a husband, Linc. Guilty by association."

"But we're cell mates. I'm one of them, one of the women."

"With a cock."

"Marilyn!" I quickly looked at the kids to see if they'd heard.

"Sorry."

"You're bad."

"You need to cook for them," she said. "As in a luncheon."

"They won't come."

"In the safety of my house? They'll come. . . . They know you can cook. I've told them."

Marilyn offered to pay for the meal. I accepted as payment for bailing her out at the dinner party. Five minutes later, however, the waitress returned with the credit card and a frown of inconvenience. "Your card's been rejected," she said. "You got another?"

"No. Just the one. Looks like you're buying, Linc. Sorry."

As we drove out of the mall parking lot, headed back home, I offered to stop by the ATM machine at the bank.

"That wouldn't do any good. I'm out of my money. I get more on Thursday."

"What do you mean, 'You get more money'?"

"From Steven."

"Is he on a monthly payroll schedule like Josephine? I can relate."

"Steven gives me my money on the first of every month."

"He rations your money?"

"He's a pilot. All pilots are assholes. They have these visions of kept wives in the castles as they zip across the kingdoms of the world."

"I can't believe he rations your money. I wouldn't stand for it."

Marilyn looked straight ahead, through the windshield. She'd just done something I'd never seen a woman do. She refreshed her tomato-colored lipstick without a mirror, the result as precise as the painted mouth of a china doll. Her lips looked like a fresh wound, that warm, inner-body red against skin that lives in climate control.

knew I'd gained weight since being at home, but I had no idea how much until the day of my interview with Robins and Fischer. I could barely button the pants of my suit, and the jacket definitely would have to stay open.

Before leaving, I left instructions for Patty to complete in her time here at least two games of Candy Land—and not to let Violet win. Candy Land is a game of chance, no skill required. I wanted Violet to learn the difference.

I met the COO in the company's offices in the Xerox tower downtown. Though he hadn't been aware of it, he was already familiar with some of my work, most notably the hedge job at the San Francisco Museum of Modern Art. He was as knowledgeable of landscaping as I. We discussed the climate of the Northeast and sap flow and hardiness zones and hybrids of maples being developed at the University of Amsterdam. It felt good talking to someone about adult matters from my previous life. I felt like an American traveling abroad who runs into another American and, homesick, enthusiastically talks about the culture he misses back home.

"What do you know about the grafting plan with the Brazilian pepper?" he asked.

"Nothing, I'm afraid."

"At the University of Miami?"

"No."

"It's been the ethical discussion in every trade journal for two or three months. Where have you been hiding?"

And I proceeded to tell him about my life the past five months. The move, the potty training, the late nights for Jo, my attempts to grow cilantro in the basement, my troubles with Patty. I went on and on, and he just sat there, listening, nodding his head, smiling at times.

"You're a busy man," he finally said.

"Extremely."

"May I ask you . . . If you don't like the nanny, why don't you replace her?"

"Have you ever had to find a nanny?" I asked.

He shook his head. "My wife takes care of that."

He looked at his watch, suddenly growing serious, and leaned over his desk, onto his elbows, folding his hands into a here-is-the-church-and-here-is-the-steeple.

"Mr. Menner, I don't believe in wasting people's time, so let me be brief."

"Okay . . ."

"Your credentials are incredible and your work impressive, but I don't think you can handle this job at this time in your life. You've got too much going on, and the demands of your wife's job are pulling on you and your energies. I have to have someone who can live and breathe this job only. In a nutshell, I need someone who has someone like you at home."

"You're kidding me," I said.

He shook his head. "Call me when things settle down, when your daughter gets into school maybe, and when you get some good help hired."

"This is discrimination," I said.

"Of what kind?"

"I'm not sure. . . . But I think it sucks."

"Timing is everything, Mr. Menner. This is not a good time for you."

"It sure isn't."

He was right, of course, and as I drove home I wondered why I'd dug into this new role so deeply. I had the key to these shackles, so what the hell was I still doing at home?

Part of it was Jo. This job consumed her as no other had, and she could contribute nothing at home. But I could not blame her entirely. Something else kept me from jumping into the swift current of the working world. Though I often pouted about being stuck at home, I also found the job vaguely satisfying. It was like running a biosphere, playing God, matter constantly moving in and out, unpredictable life forces and emotions and elements of nature all exerting their pressure, and me having to predict and anticipate and steer all this change, all this energy. I maintained the balance, lubricating all that was sluggish, nourishing and feeding and filling, introducing the new and eliminating the superfluous in my family's collective life.

And I could not ignore the aesthetic value of the job. A house is a constantly changing work of art, and it was I and

I alone who got to decide what it looked like. No client with bad taste could ruin the final product. As a person obsessed with visual details, this was no small thing.

Driving east on the 490 expressway, I passed a billboard advertising strawberries at Hi-Valu Supermarket.

Which reminded me: *Search on-line for balsamic vinegar.*

Which reminded me: *Berries. Pick up Jo's red suit at dry cleaners.*

Which reminded me: *Make appointment for Jo to see doctor about inflamed mole on neck.*

I love that neck. I miss that neck.

Her daughter has that very same neck.

The neck of a bride.

Would Violet get married?

Why did I get married?

Buy caulk for bathtub.

When did I last see Jo in a bubble bath?

Date: Tues. 5 Dec.

From: BooksBirmingham@infi.edu

To: LincolnM@aol.com

Lincoln: I called your father the other night and I hung up after I heard him answer. He said, "Carol, Carol is this you? Carol, damnit this isn't funny." He sounded so pitiful and sad, and then I felt bad that I hadn't left him a freezer full of roast-beef sandwiches and quiches like I usually do when I leave town. Do you know how he's eating? Is it dairy queen hamburgers every night like I imagine? Today in a mental state I called Charles (Charles Wyndham, do you remember him? He's the man with the perennial nursery out on Old Chaney Road) and talked to him awhile. Lincoln you need to know that Charles and I slept together. . . . . but only once, and it wasn't that great of an experience. He's my dear friend and we never should have done it.—I know it's not really fair or kind to tell you this, but it happened and I have to tell somebody. Sorry. E-mail confession. Computer monitor as priest. . . . I just needed to know what it was like to sleep with another man, if they all just poke in and out twenty times then roll over and fall asleep. I feel like a vegetable garden when I make love with your father. Once a week whether he wants it or not he dutifully positions himself between the rows and fertilizes then goes to bed feeling like he's done his job. he doesn't even smile or say anything, just kisses my cheek as if he's switching off a light.

I'm a terrible mother for telling you things like this: Yikes! I'm going to press erase instead of send . . . no mother should subject her child to this drivel.

I stopped today to visit Carol Ho; she's now the art director at Southern Living and she just got a divorce. We had dinner, and she was very encouraging of my trip. my flight? my fancy? She asked me, "are you thelma or louise?" I couldn't decide, but then I decided the former because I think brad pitt is beautiful. Why am I telling you all this? Why am I giving you such a cross to bear? Forgive me, dear, for pressing send. . . . . .

I'd also received a piece of spam from Paula's Pussy Palace: *Thousands of images of red hot women doing just what you want them to.*

What the hell, I thought, and I clicked on the blue hotlink. Paula's voice started dripping from my speakers. "Hey, Gorgeous. Let me and my girls make you happy. We accept Visa and MasterCard and your big, hard cock."

It had been awhile since I'd heard the word, and mine began stirring with life at the sound of it. I'd wondered more than once whether I was still alive down there, wondered if my lack of desire was tied more to simple exhaustion or confusion from my daily walk on that fence that separates *X* from *Y*.

The tiny classified ad came as a surprise. Jo's hospital, wanting to relandscape the entire campus, was calling for bids. I asked her about it that night over fish tacos, which I made from grouper marinated in mojo criollo then grilled over mesquite wood chips.

"You know you can't have that job, Lincoln," she said.

"What do you mean? You know my work, you know

how good I am. I'm probably the most talented landscape
architect in western New York."

"That doesn't matter," she said. "I can't give you that
job."

"You mean you don't want to."

"You're my husband, Linc. It's conflict of interest."

"The best man should win."

"I can't do it, Lincoln."

Jo took a bite of taco, and a grayish chunk of grouper
tumbled out of the shell and down her blouse. I quickly
dabbed my cloth napkin in water and went for the stain. If
I could get it out right then, I wouldn't have to wash the
blouse, which meant I wouldn't have to iron it, which
would save me twenty minutes.

"You're losing respect for me, aren't you?" I said. "I
can tell. You don't respect what I'm doing here."

"You're wrong. But I will tell you this." She reached
across the table and put her hand on mine. "I miss my
happy, cocky man," she said. "I don't even know you anymore. You're paranoid and self-conscious and you have no
self-esteem. And Lincoln . . . You're not much fun to be
around these days. You drag me down, and I have enough
dragging me down at work."

Occupational hazards, I thought, by-products of staying home with children in a world of no feedback. I looked
down at the napkin in my lap. One of its edges was beginning to fray.

Get new napkins.

Wouldn't a picnic be great right now?

How much more of this snowy weather can I take?

"Please, Lincoln, I just can't handle this discussion to-day. I just need to get some sleep."

Unconsciously, Jo wrapped her arms around herself. Was she cold? In need of a hug? She seemed so drained now, an empty olive-oil bottle. Was it my fault? I have this theory, that we abandon our bodies in times of stress. Our psyches jump ship, travel elsewhere, searching for solutions that will stabilize us, make us whole again. For much of the past five months, Jo had been gone. Somewhere. I really hadn't seen or talked to her since moving to Rochester. She had seemed like a ghost, a restless spirit making cameo appearances at the dinner table, the bathroom sink, the toilet, and then gone again. Sometimes, when she seems to be floating, her mind back at the hospital and her empty body sitting before me, I walk over, pull her to her feet and hug her long and tight, running my hands across her back, creating warmth from friction. It is physical re-suscitation. Reaching for her hand somewhere up there in the ether, yanking her back home if only for a minute.

"I'm sorry," I said. "You're right, it wouldn't look right for me to have that job."

I stood and walked over to her, took her arms and pulled her from the sofa, then dipped down, picked her up and carried her to the bedroom, something she wouldn't let me do even on our honeymoon. Historically, Jo has not been one to accept acts of chivalry, though in these past few, confusing gender-bender months, she seems to have become more accepting—needy?—of those stereotypical male-dominant actions we've always avoided. She will let me open doors for her now, and lately she's been asking me to drive when we go somewhere as a family. Now that I think of it, however, maybe it's me who has avoided these cliché male acts, and maybe I'm the one craving them now as I scan my landscape for elusive morsels of maleness.

I laid her on the bed. I unbuttoned her blouse and pulled it from her arms, then unzipped and removed her skirt, then peeled from her legs the hose that always remind me of sausage casing.

I had planned on telling her about my depressing day, but she fell into deep sleep within a minute of my setting her down. It probably was best; days do not get any worse than this. That morning, for no particular reason, I had started driving through the streets of Pittsford, up Washington Road, left onto Schoen Place, down Main Street and over to the newer developments on the southern edge of town. Patty was with Violet. I'd left instructions on how to cut out and count triangles from construction paper then glue them into some sort of mammal. "And make it a mammal," I said. "We've been learning about mammals."

Off Sunset Road, I found a cul-de-sac of houses so new that none of them had landscaping, the only sign of trees being pine dust left over from the buzz saws. In one of the driveways a man in jeans and flannel shirt unloaded firewood from a white Toyota pickup.

I pulled up to the curb, at the same time leaning over and plucking a business card from the glove compartment.

"Beautiful home," I said, walking up the driveway.

"Yeah . . . thanks," he replied. "You need something?"

"Actually I think I can help you here," I replied.

"I've only got two more loads, but thanks anyway."

"I mean with the landscaping," I said, holding out my card. "I'm the best in town."

He looked at the card then handed it back. "No thanks."

"But I can make this home look a hundred thousand more expensive."

"I said no thanks."

"You sure?"

"Yeah . . . so have a good day."

The next house was vacant, but I rang the bell of the third, and a woman answered the door.

"My name is Linc Menner. I'm a landscape architect. I was wondering if I could give you a quote on making your yard the envy of the neighborhood."

"Oh, I don't think so. No."

"Are you just going to leave it bare?"

"It's December. What do you think?"

"I think now's the time to plan that perfect backyard."

"I think I'm not interested."

"How about a row of junipers to block that nosy neighbor's view?"

She shut the door in my face. It was obvious the Amway approach was not going to work. People had grown wary of unsolicited sales calls in the fifteen years since I started my landscape business.

I tried three other houses with no success. What was wrong with me? Should I have worn a nicer shirt? Maybe I should have shaved. Was I talking in an okay-sweetheart-let's-eat-all-your-carrots-now tone? Was it obvious to them that all cockiness and confidence had fled my personality months ago? Was my stint at home dulling my edge that had cut me such a wide swath of success in the past?

I decided to try once more before returning home, a nouveau Tudor on Willisby Lane that could benefit greatly from perennial beds on both sides of the porch.

I pulled up in front of the house, turned off the ignition and sat in the dark cab of my truck, waiting, like some reluctant stalker, trying to talk myself into walking up and ringing the bell.

I could not do it. I could not handle any more rejection. I returned home, to my cage and refuge, where I was needed.

We awoke to discover that the water heater had gurgled its last breath some time that night. Since Jo had a full bathroom in her office suite, she left early to shower and dress at work. I decided to replace the heater myself and I knew my morning would be easier if I removed it before Violet woke up.

I was carrying the metal carcass up the basement stairs, my arms wrapped around it in a bear hug, when I stepped on Malibu Beach Barbie. My foot slipped a step, and instead of dropping the heater as I should have done I leaned back, trying to regain my balance, refusing to let go. With no free arms for ballast, I overshot the center of gravity and fell backwards down five or six stairs with the heater on top of me. I passed out for five minutes or so, awakened by what I thought was water, gritty and copper-smelling, dripping on my face.

Marilyn drove us to the emergency room at Westside Mercy, Genesee's competition, which was closer to our house. As they sewed sixteen stitches in my forehead and taped my left ankle, she called Jo to tell her what had happened.

Two hours later, we pulled up to the house and found Jo's Saab in the driveway. She heard us, appeared at the doorway and ran out to help Marilyn steady me into the house.

"I think I'm hallucinating," I said.

"Don't be a smart-ass," Jo replied. "Quit making me feel like a total failure."

I wasn't sure why she'd come. I could cook and take care of Violet alone, even with a bad ankle and head full of stitches. Yet over the past several months I'd learned about the power of mommy guilt, the eating away at women who are not there to nurture their loved ones as well as they'd like to, so I decided to lie still and let this inexplicable, foreign hurricane of domesticity run its course.

She dismissed Marilyn—"I can't thank you enough. I'm glad Lincoln has acquaintances in the neighbor-hood."—then set me up on the couch with some hot tea and my feather pillow. She then took Violet with her to Wegmans and Borders and returned with a stack of magazines for me and two sacks of groceries. For lunch, Jo made Kraft macaroni and cheese and canned peaches.

"I don't think Violet's ever had an all-orange meal," I said.

"I don't want to hear it, Lincoln. You're not in control today."

During Violet's nap, Jo opened the mail, dealt with the plumber and did three loads of laundry. I said nothing about her technique, though it killed me to watch her throw the white pillowcases in with blue jeans. I gave her a list of errands—dry cleaners, super glue at Kmart, Dimetapp on sale at Walgreens, plant fertilizer at Ace Hardware—and she finished them all by three o'clock. She'd been going like crazy for four hours, yet she burst through the door with that happy, messianic energy that radiates from people who have stepped in to help.

Later, Jo pulled out the ladder to rescue Tillie, who was meowing from atop the trellis in the backyard. Jo didn't know that Tillie did this to get food, that she could get down by herself quite easily. It was very sweet watching this rescue, like eavesdropping on children as they play make-believe.

She also baked two batches of cookies, the slice-and-bake variety you buy in those salami-shaped plastic tubes, and let Violet eat them an hour before dinner. She played Barbies with Violet on the floor. She took out the trash and sorted the recyclables. At the end of the day, after boiling hot dogs and cleaning the kitchen, Jo lay down beside me on the couch and closed her eyes. She still was wearing the blue Chiquita banana sticker Violet had pressed onto her forehead.

"I'm exhausted," she said. "You do all this every day. I don't see how."

"Is Violet in bed yet?"

"Mmmm," she said, nodding. "That made it all worthwhile. I love putting her to bed."

Back home in southern California, I constantly got angry at the amount of time I spent in traffic. One week I made the mistake of adding up the hours—twenty-six—I sat in my car during a five-day period. You get mad when you realize all that time could be spent on something productive or pleasurable, and you feel as if you've been robbed of something precious. This is also how I feel about bedtime with Violet.

From beginning to end, the process devours nearly ninety minutes every night, *nine* hours a week, from running the water to washing the hair to letting her play in the tub to drying to teeth-brushing to dressing to reading and singing and talking. Even if Jo is gone all day, if she can make it home for bedtime duty my life and morale improves dramatically. Ninety minutes of free time! What should I do with it? Read? Take a bath? Wash the white load? Everyone wins if Jo gets home in time for bedtime duty, especially Jo, because for her it is a sweet, novel experience, like discovering a litter of puppies beneath the porch. The rocking, the singing and reading the books, the sitting on the toilet, talking with each other during the bath. When Jo puts Violet to bed, she walks into the kitchen afterward looking dreamily sedate and emotionally overwhelmed.

Stuck on the couch, my wife in my arms and no demand calling my name, I traced *passiflora*'s progress as far as possible from my vantage point. As I predicted, my vine eventually had tired of its travels through the dining room and wandered into the doorway of the kitchen. I had repotted the plant and bought two goldfish whose nitrogen-rich water was poured exclusively on *passiflora*. By my estimations it would reach the living room, then maybe return to its roots in the dining room, by Valentine's Day. So remarkable was its progress that I'd called a professor in the horticulture department at the University of Rochester, though I never heard from him. Angry at first, I mellowed when I tried to visualize the message his secretary might have written: . . . *has passion plant growing all over house, thought you might be interested.*

Evidently, Jo was not sleeping. "What is it about the damned plant, Lincoln?" she asked.

"I don't know," I said. "I can't explain it."

"Try. For me, please. Try."

"I like to chart its growth."

"Why?"

"I don't see progress anymore."

"Violet's not progress?"

"Numbers. I need numbers. Dollar figures. Tallies of sales contracts, bags of cypress mulch. I'm not doing so well in my world here, Jo. I can't measure my success."

I walked in from the groccry store, crinkly bags suspended from my arms like hangers on a rod, and found Violet and Patty watching *The Little Mermaid.*

"Where did you find that movie?" I asked.

"In your underwear drawer," Patty said, unable to pull herself from the screen.

"What the hell were you doing in my underwear drawer?"

"Violet asked me to get it out."

"And so you did what a child ordered you to do? Did you not think for a second that the reason this stinking movie is not included with the others in the armoire is because I don't want her to see it?"

Finally, she looked away from the television and up at me. "What the frick? What's wrong with this? It's Disney for chrissakes."

"It's poison. Patty, you've got to get better at monitoring what goes into Violet. You know how picky I am about her diet. I'm just as picky about her mental diet. . . . Put in *Pocahontas.*"

Though the animators caught absolute hell for giving

her Barbie's va-va-voom measurements, Pocahontas reigns supreme. I like everything about her: her knowledge of plant life, awareness of the biosphere and where she fits into it. Respect for her father. Curiosity of things unknown. The courage to challenge a male-dominant culture. The integrity needed to leave her lover behind and stay with her people because they need her more than he. On the flip side is Ariel in *The Little Mermaid*. No redeeming traits. Zero. She continually defies her father and wants nothing more than to be some rich hunk's bride. I cheer for Ursula, the sea witch who enslaves her.

Pocahontas on play, I sat down in my office to check my e-mail. Again, nothing from my California friends. It would be unfair to expect them to suddenly be frequent letter writers; I'd told them for years that I never read their e-mails, and that they shouldn't spend their time sending them because I did not have the time or inclination to respond. Nowadays, however, I find myself more needy of communication.

I did have three new arrivals: a summer clear-out notice from L. L. Bean, a string of housewife jokes from my aunt Jean in Bakersfield, and the most recent flee-and-tell entry from my mother.

> *Date: Fri. 3 Jan.*
> *From: DallasMetroLibraries@Tex.rmi.edu*
> *To: LincolnM@aol.com*
> *I spent the afternoon quick-painting people's portraits on McKibbon Boulevard, not far from THE grassy*

*knoll. Economic indicator: Women carrying Talbots or
Neiman Marcus bags will pay $75 for a five-minute
drawing of their little darlings.*

*I'm still intrigued as to why americans so revere
JFK anyway. I'm guessing it's because he died before we
could rummage through his closet. . . . . It's
much like marriage: We all marry a beautiful, wonderful door, and, for a while anyway, just looking at that
door pleases us all enough. What solid strength! What
grain! What lovely curves on the door handle! Then we
get bored and we open it and start poking around inside. On a long and fascinating journey, we see the dust,
the interesting dents in the baseboards, the shoes that
don't fit, the ties and clothes and fashions from another
era, and the skeletons of course. . . . . This was NOT the
case with your father. I found NOTHING inside your
father's closet. . . . nothing at all. It was empty. I guess
he should be commended for his outer facade telling
the complete and honest story . . . like a solid, steel
I-beam. . . . . beauty in simplicity . . . but you know me
well enough to know that I need complexity, and if I
don't find it I will create it. So here I am. I've needed
something more complex and satisfying and tasty for
such a long time. . . . . I stayed. But I got tired of sacrificing, especially when I realized one day—the prover-
bial light bulb—that your father hadn't sacrificed one
thing in his life. His long hours at the dealership are not
torture, as you probably are well aware. He LIVES for
work. He LOVES his work. Does he ask about me?*

*More on Dallas: I remember reading a new york
times piece years ago about all the bleached big hair in
dallas and wowsa is it true. I'm also fascinated by that
big orblike thing downtown . . . reminds me of a cat's
penis. You did know, didn't you, that the male cat's penis is spiked, and withdrawal from the poor female is
excruciatingly painful . . . evidently the pain sparks
ovulation. Maybe God's a man after all.*

*I wish I could talk to you. . . . I guess I could call but
for some reason I like this hiding in cyberspace. It's a
nice puffy, safe buffer. It's like I'm god or a conscience
or something. Jiminy Cricket! It's really kind of interesting. . . . No?*

I miss my kitchen and my jade plant. Love you.

She seemed to be in a hurry, like a dog who has escaped
from the fenced yard and hungrily sniffs as much of the
neighborhood as possible because he knows this sweet
freedom will be brief.

My father would be incapable of such tangential
thought, even in a from-the-hip e-mail. I'm sure this is
partly why she can drive him so crazy, partly why, I now
realize, he spent so much time away from the house, working. My father has a place for everything, a compartment
for each key chain, emotion, pair of shoes and pliers. My
mother the artist thinks the way a mosquito flies. Where are
my keys? Where's my purse? Has anyone seen my check-
book? Are they over here? Over here? Over there? Imagine

what a household looks like when it's run by someone like
this. Needless to say, things accumulate—the way they
never will accumulate in my house—so slowly you hardly
notice, like the way calcium deposits form on the outside of
a faucet. I don't know how many times I heard, "Don't
touch that, it's a still life." I know this is why my father
spends most of his time at the office. He hires a janitor,
but my father still does much of the cleaning. It's his orderly
home. Walking through Menner's Ford-Lincoln-Mercury,
even the body shop, you'd never guess there was grease or
oil in a car. I remember one Thanksgiving afternoon when
I was sent to find him, and there he was in his underwear
and shirt and tie, scrubbing the gray painted floor on his
hands and knees. His pants were neatly draped over the
back of a crushed velvet front seat in a Lincoln on the
showroom floor. This was the first time I stopped to notice
what a strange mix of a marriage it really was.

The first time I asked Mom about her marriage was
about twelve years ago, before I married Jo. She called me
in Palm Springs, where I'd just been hired by a reputable
landscaper.

"I was wondering how you were doing," she said on the
phone. "I mean, could you stand some company for a few
days?"

"What happened?" I asked.

"Your father's trying to tell me how to vote again. I'm
just sick of it. He's so damn Republican it just makes me
sick. He was reading the paper today, something about a

gay pride parade in Chicago, and he made some comment about the—quote—little faggots, and it made me mad."

"Mom," I asked her, "if you're that ideologically different then why in the hell did you marry him?"

"I don't know, Lincoln. Your father was adorable. He drove a convertible. He hasn't always been like this. Something happened along the way, like he saw Medusa and turned to stone. Your father does not react, Lincoln."

Yet they lived together, as many unhappy couples do from that era—because starting over, starting anything over, takes too much courage and optimism and time and energy. I liken it to the American consumer with the first wave of Japanese cars that rolled into California during the energy crisis of the early seventies. Though the imports found popularity, a sizable minority of consumers refused to try them because the marriage they'd had with their Buicks and Chevrolets was just fine, thank you, and what on earth could they gain from switching? Loyalty is xenophobia in disguise. My father has never switched brands of shampoo (Prell, which is getting very difficult to find) or toothpaste (regular Colgate) in his life. My mother is another story. I remember the night she came home after test-driving a Honda Civic. "How could you do this to me?" my father asked. "Don't you have any loyalty?" Ebullient with praise, she implored him to open a Honda dealership. He refused, of course, though I'm certain he now regrets this mistake; Blankenship Honda in Bakersfield is the most profitable Honda dealership in California. My mother, of course, shared this information with me when she read it in the *Bakersfield Times-Ledger*.

Yet I also know she would wither if left alone. My father is as steady and strong as a Savannah live oak. My mother knows he will always be there, which is critical if you know how, as a child, she was passed from parent to parent to uncle to aunt to parent. I've seen childhood movies of my mother running from *A* to *F* to *B* to *X*, never linear, never walking, arms flailing every which way like tentacles gone mad. Too much energy, too many questions. She must have worn them all out. It might have been the world's first experiment in tag-team parenting. Thus, my mother's fear of abandonment is so extreme that if she drops a pea down the garbage disposal she quickly dispatches another so it does not feel alone. Instinctively, I knew she could not venture out into the world alone.

I signed off and called Dad

"Is Mom's computer on?"

"I don't know. Yeah, I guess so. Why?"

I pictured the dark den with the Flintstones screensaver flickering on the walls.

"Did you ever think she might be sending e-mails?"

"Why won't she just call?"

"Doesn't want to confront you, I guess. Go check the e-mails."

"I don't know how to do that."

"You don't get e-mails at work?"

"Doris takes care of it all and prints them out for me."

"Go over and sit down at the computer, Dad."

"Why?"

"Just go over and sit down in front of the keyboard. . . . Okay, hit the space bar. Now, double-click on the little envelope."

I hoped to God she'd sent him different messages than the ones she'd been sending me.

"Jo, can you help me?" I asked, walking into the bathroom. She sat on the toilet, panties down to her ankles, her legs slathered in shaving cream. Her focus continually shifted from the gliding razor to the computer-generated spreadsheet that lay on the floor. My wife is incapable of doing one thing at a time. I blame this on her overachieving father, a steamroller of a man who not only was pharmacist in town but also farmed six thousand acres of citrus outside Tulare. Like Violet, Jo was an only child, and every expectation was loaded solely upon her shoulders. I'm sure this is why she wants another child.

The way she multitasks! It's as if her father, now dead, is standing behind her, shaking his finger—*Josephine, you can do MORE, MORE, MORE, MORE!*—his finger beating the air like a metronome, setting the predictable but frenetic pace for her life. I remember very clearly the day we were driving away from our wedding, for a weekend over in Half Moon Bay. She sat in her wedding dress, not only peeling an orange but also driving and navigating with an open road atlas in her lap, verbally concocting a business plan for my soon-to-be landscaping company.

"Are you pooping or shaving?" I asked.

"Both. What do you need?"

"I need to know what to wear today."

"Your luncheon with the girls."

"Come off it, Jo. I don't have much that fits."

She reached out and patted my naked stomach. What used to be relatively flat now rounded outward at about the same arc as the top of a warm muffin.

"You are so cute I can't stand it."

"Don't do that," I said. "I hate that. I feel bad enough about myself."

"I'm just amazed at how big it's gotten. It's a dad gut."

"Enough, okay? What do I wear? What will they wear?"

"They'll be dressy, shopping-at-the-Galleria casual."

"And . . ."

"And I think you should wear blue jeans and a nice top. How about the red one from Mexico with the hood?"

I shook my head. "I'm fixing a Mexican salad and I don't want it to look like I'm doing some sort of schmaltzy theme luncheon."

"Then how about your black turtleneck?"

"With this?" I asked, patting my gut.

"Lincoln, all their husbands have bellies. Look around. These are guys who mow their own yards on Saturday for exercise. . . . Just don't tuck it in."

Dressed in what Jo suggested, I loaded all my perishables into three Mexican beach bags and trudged through the snow to Marilyn's, Violet on my back. Marilyn had decided the lunch would be less threatening if it were on neutral ground, and I was glad she'd done so. The day before

I'd spent six hours driving from one Asian grocery to another, looking for fresh cherimoyas. Cleaning my own house would have nudged me over the edge.

Cherimoya.

I'm Chiquita Banana, and I'm here to say.

Vacation in the tropics.

Buy new winter coat for Violet.

Me in a swimming suit.

Was Jo still attracted to me?

Don't be so negative.

Pick up photos from Walgreens.

Smiling in pictures.

Remember to smile.

Marilyn was dressed in black pants and a silver-gray turtleneck sweater that clinged to her like Saran Wrap around raw meat. So intentionally highlighted and dominant were the curves of her body that I feared a compliment directed toward anything from the neck down would be misconstrued as flirting and desire.

Violet scampered downstairs to watch a video. "I like your earrings," I said.

"Oh," she replied, touching her ears as if she'd forgotten they were there. "Thanks."

"You ready to get to work?"

"How about some wine?"

"It's eight in the morning, Marilyn."

"I know—I'm getting a late start."

"How much wine do you go through in a week?" I asked.

"That depends."

"On."

"How much Steven is around."

"Where is he now."

"Salmon fishing in Minnesota."

"But he just got back from a long Tokyo haul, right?"

"Notice a pattern here?"

"You think he's got another woman somewhere?"

We were standing at the kitchen counter. She shrugged her shoulders, folding a cloth napkin, pressing hard enough at the seams that she forced the blood from her fingertips. Marilyn has this habit, folding things—napkins, a sheet of uncooked, fresh pasta, a note card with a grocery list—into extinction. It always reminds me of those last few seconds of a LifeSaver on the warm, wet tongue before it disappears. Something closing down, fade to black, and the ensuing tug-of-war between satisfaction and longing. It's obvious to me that she wants something to disappear.

"I have a theory," she said. "You wanna hear it? My gay theory?"

"What?"

"I have this theory that most men are gay and they don't even know it."

"Say what?"

"Of course, they don't know it because—no offense here—they're not the most enlightened creatures on the planet, so they convince themselves they want to poke pussy, and they get married, and they procreate and get that good ol' family name out there into the world, and then they lose interest because they've done their job."

"That is dark and weird, Marilyn."

"Then why are there so many unfulfilled wives? Why do so many husbands ignore their wives' emotional needs?"

"Because man was not meant to be monogamous," I said. "That's my theory."

"But you're not like that. . . . Are you?"

"No," I answered. "You're right. I'm not like that."

I silently toasted my mom, the woman who raised me as the Anti-Dad, the boy who would grow up to be sensitive and expressive, the opposite of the man she loved no more. The dolls and bake sets, the lectures on the importance of helping my lovers achieve orgasm. She constantly let it be known that women had shitty, dismal lives, and it was my job to understand and help. We couldn't even watch a movie together without commentary: "You know why she feels unfulfilled, don't you?" Being a man should be easy, but it's not for me because I know too much. I've crossed over too many times, offense studying the defense.

"Frankly I don't give a shit if he's here or not," Marilyn continued. "I have more fun when he's not, and when he is here, all he does all day long is try to second-guess my parenting skills. And he walks around the house, trying to notice what's new so he can ask me how much it cost."

We set about cutting and dicing ingredients on her

butcher block, which I covet; the size of a card table, it can hold four large pizza pies. I then assembled into a Dutch oven, a mixture of chicken thighs, cubes of lamb, garlic, dried apricots, shiny kalamata olives, tamarind paste, fresh thyme and rosemary, then, finally, salt and fresh-ground pepper.

"What are you going to use for liquid?" Marilyn asked.

"Don't you think the olive oil will be enough?"

She shook her head, walked over and poured two gloogs of chardonnay into the pot. "It'll help take the bite off the tamarind."

For a salad, I tossed watercress, baby spinach and dandelion greens with a dressing I made from balsamic vinegar, pureed cherimoya and walnut oil. I would pair with this Linc's renowned sourdough bread, accompanied by unsalted butter, all in all, a simple meal but complex in flavor.

They arrived in twos, as if too intimidated to come alone. I recognized them all from the playground and their cars, though of course they pretended they'd never seen me. They had to because they *had* seen me—I'm not stupid!—shifting their attention to the backseat or the rearview mirror whenever we passed each other at five miles an hour. Even Mirabel Steiner, the do-goody woman from the playground who mistook me for a child molester, claimed ignorance, until I reminded her that we had indeed met.

As my entrée simmered, Marilyn poured wine for them

all. To be polite, I'm sure, they honed in on landscaping and tried to grow a conversation around it, and for the next thirty minutes, like some host on a radio call-in program, I answered their questions about house plants and gardening. Eventually, the conversation turned from my life to theirs and meatier, more pertinent matters: an overly harsh second-grade teacher at Allendale Elementary . . . the class-action lawsuit against Chrysler and its minivans . . . how the Target at Perinton was better than the one at Penfield.

Violet pattered into the room. "Excuse me," she boomed, stopping the conversation. "Daddy, can I please have some chocolate milk?"

"Violet, you're interrupting," I said. "Please apologize. And next time, wait until you hear a lull in the conversation."

"I'm sorry," she said. "I need some milk, Daddy."

"Sure, hon, come into the kitchen. You have to drink it in the kitchen."

"No she doesn't," Marilyn said.

"It's a rule of mine, Marilyn."

A few minutes later, she walked past us, back toward the basement steps. "Thank you, Daddy," she said, then scampered out of the room and down the stairs, back to Dax and Sarah and the *Rescuers Down Under* video.

"Is she always like that?" asked Linda Boatright, gray Volvo sedan.

"Always," Marilyn answered.

"It must be a man's voice," said Leah Redmondson, metallic-tan Navigator. "I think children react more to a man's voice. It's stronger, scarier."

"I don't think that's it at all." I must have sounded perturbed because every mother at the table immediately began darting their eyes from woman to woman, measuring each other's reaction: *Oh, my God, what's he going to say?*

"I've worked hard for that behavior," I said. "I got that behavior through consistent praise and setting of limits and expectations."

"I didn't mean to offend you," Leah said. "I'm sure you do a good job. I just sometimes wonder if there's this primal thing about a man's voice."

"I've got my own theory," said Nan Phipps, black Mercedes station wagon. "I have a good friend, a man, who's home with the kids, just as you are, Linc. And his kids are the same way. Sweet, obedient. I think it's because men are more selfish than women, they have less patience, and they refuse to put up with all the bullshit that we put up with. What do you think, Linc? Does it ring true?"

I thought of all the times when Violet's lips would begin to tremble, and my bearish, staccato uh-uh-uh-uh-I-don't-want-to-hear-it-Vi-let would immediately extinguish any tiny flames of a fit. Jo has said I'm teaching her to supress her feelings. What she doesn't know is that when a good, hard cry is called for, when it is necessary salve for a badly stubbed toe or when she misses her mommy, I let her cut loose. We've even had crying contests in the family room, lying on our backs, staring up at the twenty-foot-high ceiling, taking turns screaming and wailing as loudly as we can. I'd never realized how cathartic exaggerated crying can be, a total, full-throttle gallop ending with exhaustion, energy tanks drained and a tingling in the extremities. Much like an orgasm.

"You might have a point there, Nan," I said.

"Did you guys know my friend applied to be the leader for his daughter's Brownie troop?" Nan asked.

"You're kidding," Leah said.

"And they won't let him. Apparently it's against regulation."

"Duh! What did he expect?" Leah said.

"But Cub Scout troops have den *mothers*," I said.

"Yes . . . But that's different," Leah said.

"How? You tell me how that's different. That is just closed-minded as hell."

Again, the women all looked at one another: *Oh my God, he's mad! Who's going to tell him the truth?*

"Face it, Linc. Can you remember a female child molester?" Marilyn said. They all nodded their heads.

"Okay, you might be different, Linc," Nan said. "But put yourself in another dad's shoes. Would you want Violet's Brownie leader to be a man? Other than yourself, I mean."

Indeed, I'd always instructed Violet to seek a female stranger if she ever were to get lost in the mall or on a downtown street. My little girl with a male stranger? Of course the answer was no. I belong to the criminal, predatory gender, one of those who crawled from the cauldron of testosterone. I believe that men's boiling libidos are genetically set; there's a reason a man can ejaculate every fifteen minutes. It was God's intention for the prick to be a tireless population-building tool. Yet in the past five hundred years we've been trying to tame it, which is akin to quieting the churning, red-hot volcanic activity in the bowels of the earth: It can't be done. This is why that poor guy is not allowed to be the leader of his daughter's Brownie troop. This is why, when we make a play date with a new friend, the mother drops the child off, sees there's no mother at home, then suddenly decides she has a free two-hour chunk of time to sit and talk and watch the girls play.

I should have tucked my tail—my cock?—between my legs and agreed, but I had to defend my gender, pitiful as it may be.

"No, I have to disagree with you," I said, looking at Leah. "I think some men can do a better job than women."

Leah shook her head and laughed. Laughed! "How can you say that?" she asked.

Obviously I knew by now this friendship would not be a good fit, so I let 'er rip. "How can I say it? I'll tell you how I can say it. Who's on top of the snow mountain playing with your kids for an hour at a time? Who's pushing the merry-go-round so you can sit on your asses and chat with your girlfriends? Who has to police the monkey bars so the big kids don't walk on the little ones' fingers? I am. It's me.

Because you don't want to drag your butt off that bench and get down and dirty with your kids."

Nan laughed, hard and out loud, quickly applying a Band-Aid to a conversation turned bloody. It was a symbolic arm, reached across the table for a man in need, and I grabbed it, knowing that, once again, I'd gone too far and said too much.

I laughed. Others joined in, though the damage had been done. I dismissed myself to assemble dessert, my flan topped with a mint-mango puree and shavings of semisweet, dark chocolate. Obviously, the rest of the meal was strained, and Marilyn's gallant attempt to mainstream me had collapsed like a fallen soufflé.

Still, they now knew that I could cook, probably better than any of them, and I took a strange pleasure in knowing that my delicious food had invaded their bodies, that these women would return home and wash their clothes and help with homework and clean the toilets, all these actions fueled by calories from food all touched by me, chicken thighs, onions, mangoes. And as this food, laced with my cells, found its way into their bloodstream, I would become part of these women, their livers and kidneys, their hair, their skin, and though their conscious minds would tell them to avoid me, the very molecular structure of their bodies would recognize me as kin.

Linc's Mediterranean Stew

SERVES FOUR

3 tablespoons olive oil

5 garlic cloves, minced

4 chicken thighs, skinned

1 pound lean lamb, cubed

1 cup white wine

4 cups chicken stock or broth

20 dried apricots

1 (7-ounce) jar kalamata olives, pitted

10 prunes (Honest: You need these to make it
good.)

1 tablespoon fresh thyme, chopped

1 tablespoon fresh rosemary, chopped
Salt and pepper

2–3 tablespoons Dijon mustard
Tamarind paste, optional

In a large pan or Dutch oven, heat oil then sauté
garlic and brown chicken on one side. Turn and add
lamb. Once brown, remove meat to plate and drain
oil. Then add wine, stirring, to dissolve particles on
bottom of pan. Add chicken broth and all other ingredients except mustard. Stir, cover and simmer
for 90 minutes, stirring occasionally. Over time, the

prunes will disintegrate and help form a nice, semi-thick sauce.

Before serving, stir in the Dijon, adding more if you want a more tangy dish. If you have tamarind paste, replace one tablespoon of the mustard with the paste. Add fresh-ground black pepper to taste.

Despite the sauvignon blanc, the mushrooms still lacked the deep, layered taste I was hoping for. These chanterelles needed extra zing because they were going to sit atop plain mashed potatoes, which can blunt and extinguish even the strongest of flavors. Cilantro wouldn't work, though parsley would help, because it was not compatible with the cream we would later add. I walked over to the refrigerator and scanned the bottles in the side door.

"Aha!" I said to Marilyn, who was peeling potatoes at the sink. "Anchovy paste."

"Perfect."

"And then, just before serving, some pecorino Romano cheese sprinkled on the top. Parmigiano-Reggiano doesn't have the bite we need."

The phone rang. It was Jo, calling to say she'd left a floppy disk—she *thought* she'd left a floppy disk—somewhere at home. Could I stop what I was doing and search for it?

Marilyn helped me comb through the house, under the bed, behind dressers, in the deep, dark slits of the upholstery. After a half hour we found it beneath a roll of toilet paper on the back of the john in the master bath. I realized

I should have looked there first. Jo reads on the toilet, writes letters on the laptop, even eats on the toilet.

"You want to go with me downtown? I need to get this to her."

"After we eat?"

"I mean now. Jo won't rest until she has this in her hands."

"Can you drive?"

"We can't fit us all into my truck."

"I meant the Suburban."

"You don't mind me driving your car?"

"I like having a man drive. But we have to stop and get the Game Boys."

"We don't need them."

"We do if we want to get any talking done."

"No we won't."

We pulled out of the driveway. I honked and waved as we passed the house of Leah Redmondson, who was out getting her mail. She closed the mailbox, ignoring me, and turned to go inside.

"You're terrible," Marilyn said. "You're antagonizing her."

"I don't care," I said. "What did she say about me after I left?"

"That you were a typical man."

"Ha!"

By the time we passed Marilyn's house, the normally boisterous, argumentative Dax and Sarah had quieted down as Meryl Streep's creamy voice filled the backseat with *Peter Cottontail*. I hate Game Boys, I hate all video games. They're nothing but drugs that anesthetize children for lazy parents, as nutritionally empty as Doritos and goldfish crackers.

Marilyn looked out the window. "I've got to get the ivy trimmed. It's driving Steven crazy."

I still had not formally met Steven, my exposure to him largely comprised of visual snippets from the vantage point of my kitchen window. Dressed in his pilot blues, I would see him getting into his truck. Just as my mother used to watch the planes from LAX ascend over our house, wishing she were on board no matter their destination, I would watch him drive away, coveting his imminent departure to some place far from home.

"The ivy's not that bad," I said.

"He's obsessed with grooming. It's a pilot thing."

I felt my own stubble with the back of my fingers, raking upward, against the whiskers like the credit card in the old Edge commercials. I needed to shave more; Jo likes me clean shaven, but I don't bother because she's rarely home by the time I go to bed.

We headed east on 490, into Rochester, gray and gritty even in the summer, home to smokestack sprawl, Kodak, Xerox, Bausch and Lomb and a chunk of dark-brown beach on Lake Ontario that frequently gets shut down because of a nasty, high-bacteria count. In these winter months the city looks like a black-and-white photograph, the low-lying steel-gray clouds pushing down on me like those heavy lead bibs the dentist lays across my chest during X rays. Obviously my environment hasn't helped my moods these past few months. I'm not accustomed to living in a place where fresh flowers are a necessary mood tonic on people's grocery-shopping lists. I can't help but think I'd be happier if I were back home, in California.

Golden gate.

Golden handcuffs.

Did Jo actually like working so hard?

Would she be home more if she wanted to?

Was I chasing her away with gloom?

Add a plant to top of entertainment armoire.

Why do we hide our televisions?

We need a new TV.

Overflowing landfills.

How long could it go on?

How long could Mom stay on the lam?

Lamb shanks for dinner?

"I can trim that ivy for you," I said.

"You can? You can get that high?"

"Yep."

"You'd do that for me?"

"Absolutely."

"That would be great. I could use the money for something else. I've been looking at Persians for the foyer."

Marilyn looked down at her open hands, then started tracing the lines in her palm with a finger as if she were consulting a map, gauging distance, finding a destination.

"We all should hate you," she said.

"Excuse me?"

"You do your own yard work. You fix your own garage door. Your house is spotless."

"Everyone's looks cleaner than your own."

"The average homemaker does not vacuum underneath the cushions of her furniture. Does Patty help?"

"I don't let her touch it. She couldn't do it the way I want her to."

"Why don't you hire a housekeeper? I'd die without Betsey."

"I can't justify the cost, I'm not making any money."

"And Jo doesn't make you feel bad about that, does she?"

"Never."

Yet I could not deny that guilt had been a persistent theme in this new life of mine. I could not help but feel guilty about having a nanny when I'm not making any money. I feel guilty about dining al fresco with a friend at a sunny table while my wife no doubt is hurriedly snarfing down a pressed-meat sandwich from a vending machine. To assuage this guilt, I've tried to make Jo high-flavor, high-protein meals that she can warm up in a microwave, but she won't even take the time to walk down one flight of stairs to the employee lounge and warm them up. I've given her tiny Tupperware containers of chopped cilantro and basil. Put this on your sandwich or in your soup, I tell her. Treat yourself. Do these little things to feed your senses and your soul. Yet I find these containers of moldy herbs rolling around on the floor of her Saab, along with the Ziploc bags of moldy carrots I cut and send with her in the morning. I know she's been eating unhealthy

vending-machine food by the number of times I find Doritos cheese dust on her dress. Why won't she take care of
herself? Am I not doing something right? My wife is not
happy. This must be my fault—but how?

I do have an occasional day when my life seems so
good that I feel guilty. I'd like to say it's a day spent playing
and reading and painting with my daughter, but it's not. It
is usually a day when Violet has a baby-sitter, and I have
no one to worry about for four hours but myself. These are
the days the beds don't get made until six o'clock. I buy a
rotisserie chicken and Tuscan green beans at the Wegmans
deli and warm and serve them that night as my own. I will
drive downtown to Newspapers of the World, where I
might buy a horticulture magazine and the previous Sunday's copy of the *L.A. Times*. I'll find an ethnic restaurant
on Monroe Avenue and sit and dine and read casually for
two hours. Then, slightly buzzed from my two beers,
knowing I should not yet drive, I might wander through
downtown, stopping into stores to look at gas grills, wine
glasses, throw pillows, mulcher mowers. I'll buy some coffee and sit down on a bench near the snow-covered splash
fountain, where in warmer months random ropes of water
spurt from holes in the ground. The first time I took Violet
here she screamed, "Daddy, the ground goes potty!" Sober
enough to drive home, I might listen to the radio station
that I myself get to choose, not Radio Disney. I'll drive with
the window open because I can. And then it hits me as it
always hits me when I spend time on myself. I feel guilty
about getting angry with my daughter because she holds

me prisoner. I feel guilty about wanting to escape her. I could have been using this time to develop her mind in some way, maybe a trip to the arboretum or digging up earth worms in the backyard. Instead, I chose to sate myself with unnecessary delights. I am selfish, a bad parent.

I feel guilty because I read the newspaper every day, yet Jo won't floss her teeth most nights or ask a waiter for fresh-ground pepper because she says it takes too much time. Huge decisions tower over her, casting a shadow that I can still sense at night when she's trying to fall asleep. While I worry about whether the afternoon sun is fading the pillows on the couch, Jo's deciding whether to fire the single mother in the X-ray lab or slash six positions in accounting or whether to evict an old woman who has lost her health insurance.

Then, as quickly as the guilt falls upon me, it disappears because the cat pees in a potted plant or Violet drops a glass of milk at the top of the stairs. Something happens that thrusts me back into the brainless, adultless world where I must dwell for most of my day—and then it is Jo who should feel guilty, not me.

I reached to turn down the volume of the Peter Rabbit tape. The part where Peter runs from Mr. McGregor and his rake, marked by a galloping of high-pitched violins, hurts my ears.

"But what's happened," I said to Marilyn, "is that I've turned into an out-of-control pleaser. I'm hyper-nurturing Jo because I feel so guilty that she's working such long hours, and she's stressed to the max in this job, she's not

happy. I can tell she's barely treading water, so I do everything. I pay the bills, buy her tampons, iron her shirts, pick
up the panties she leaves on the floor. Everything."

"You're going to resent her."

"It's already happening."

"I'm sure it is."

"I just can't get over how one unhappy person can poison an entire household," I said.

I remembered the previous night, the three of us sitting
at the table eating pasta puttanesca.

"Violet, honey, please don't suck up your noodles," I
said. "You're old enough to eat like a big girl."

I looked at Jo. "You could help me a little here. I'm tired
of being the bad guy all the time."

Later, away from Violet, she asked me to defend my
accusation.

"My parental commands are losing their punch," I
said. "They're starting to sound like background Muzak. It
would really help if you corrected her on some things."

"I do," she said.

"No, Jo, you don't. When it comes to parenting, you
take the path of least resistance."

"I'm never here, Lincoln."

"But when you are you could help a little in the standards department."

"Don't get so pissy about it. All you need to do is ask."

"No, Jo . . . I shouldn't *have* to ask. Just as I shouldn't
have to ask you to help me dry the dishes or throw your
dirty clothes in the hamper or offer to drive on long trips

because I'm exhausted from cleaning the house and packing. All I'm asking for is a little awareness of the people around you. You don't appreciate me," I said. "If you appreciated me more you'd pick up after yourself better. Do you know what it means when you throw your socks and toenail clippings on the floor? It means you don't value my time."

"I'm just one huge, goddamn failure, aren't I?"

"No. You're really good at making money and running a hospital."

Every day, the good caregiver walks that fine line, with a glass of wine in one hand and a dishrag in the other, that separates duty from personal desire. Was I asking too much? Were my expectations of Jo unfairly high? Was I standing up for myself or being an asshole? How could I expect her to take out the garbage when her boss has demanded an immediate two-million-dollar cut in operating costs?

Our relationship had hit bottom. I hadn't gotten laid in five weeks. Jo was emotionally and physically empty, a by-product of her work. I was intellectually empty, a by-product of being home with a child. There is no spark between two empty energy sources.

We have about twelve command performances each year, most of them black-tie events. I used to hate these things, but now that I'm housebound I look forward to most of them. I'm the country boy coming into the big city, a little surprised by visual details such as a martini glass and heads elegantly wrapped in turbans. For the first hour or so I tie most of what I see to things back home in my world: the woman's dress that is the color of Big Bird, the penne pasta that Violet says look like baby straws.

At home before the chamber of commerce's annual gala, Jo was putting on makeup while I combed my mustache and hair. My gut stretched the white shirt enough that the studs popped forward like metallic, outy belly buttons.

"Are you sure this thing's all right?" I asked her.

"What?"

"Am I too fat for this shirt?"

"It's fine, Linc. You're cute, like a penguin."

I set down my brush, gave myself a quick once-over, then turned to Jo. "You sure look great tonight, Lincoln," I said.

She finished brushing on her mascara before answering me. "You always compliment yourself before I get a chance to."

"And you always give that excuse," I said. "You never tell me I'm handsome. I tell you every day of the world that you're beautiful. I'd kind of like to hear the same some time."

"You're beautiful."

"I just wish you were more expressive, Jo. An unsolicited compliment never hurts."

"I tell you you're the world's greatest dad all the time," she said.

"I want you to tell me I'm gorgeous and sexy and I still

make your loins tingle. That's what I want. I'm so damned utilitarian I feel like a pack horse."

"I'm not going to say it now. You won't think it's sincere."

I picked up a Pottery Barn catalog and sat on the closed toilet to wait. I could tell she was still five minutes out.

"Are you not attracted to me anymore?" I asked.

She set down her eyeliner, walked over, laid her hands at the top of my forehead, then slowly smoothed them across my hair. She gently pulled my face into her stomach, and I wrapped my arms around her waist.

"I love you, Lincoln. I would be falling apart without you. Don't you know that?"

"I know it. I just need to see more of you."

"You didn't see much more of me in my old job."

"Yeah, but I used to have a life outside the house. You're the only grown-up friend I have now."

"What about Marilyn?"

"Marilyn's a drinking buddy. I miss *you*."

With me sitting on the toilet, Jo hugged my head, stroking my hair just as I do with Violet when she's gloomy.

"Oh, Lincoln," she whispered. "Where in the hell have you gone?"

I'd always thought confidence was as permanent as eye color or earlobe size, but it had become clear to me that it was fragile as corn chips.

"You need to put on your black underwear," I said, lifting my head and reaching for the toilet paper so I could wipe my eyes. "The white will show through."

For eight weeks I'd been dropping by, unannounced, at Empire Montessori on Pike's Bend Road. They'd grown accustomed to the big man with the beard stubble who always asked, "Would you mind if I observed a classroom?"

Marilyn teased me for being anal and overprotective, but I had to make certain the school was a good fit for Violet. I'd noticed that too many preschools seemed obsessed with protecting the child's self-esteem, which meant discipline was close to nix, which meant the atmosphere of the school would evolve over the months from a controlled simmer to an all-out flambé, and my daughter would learn nothing.

Now it was their turn to grill me. Violet and I showed up promptly at ten o'clock for our interview with Roberta Jenkinson, the headmistress. My daughter worked a puzzle on the floor as we sat in tiny chairs, my knees at sternum level.

"She's brilliant, of course," I said, smiling. "I'm sure you never hear parents say such a thing."

I'm usually excellent at eliciting response in any conversation, and I do not feel at ease unless I can get my listener to smile and loosen up. Yet it soon became obvious that Ms. Jenkinson, as her school grew in popularity with the affluent Pittsford moms, had transformed from bubbly saleswoman to judge. She looked at me with Easter Island stillness as I attempted time and again to evoke something more than a barely perceptible nod.

"She's known her letters since she was two, all of them, the whole alphabet," I said. "I found this foam alphabet at a learning store in L.A., and I throw them into the bath every night, kind of like a giant alphabet soup, and we talk about sounds of letters. Diphthongs even. Violet knows diphthongs, not all of them but a lot of them."

Nod. Nod.

"Her speech is unbelievable for a child her age. . . . Violet?"

"Yes, Daddy?"

"Please tell Ms. Jenkinson why Tillie's been banished to the outside."

Violet looked up at me, then her. "Because Tillie's been pottying in Daddy's *passiflora* and Daddy's *passiflora* will die if it gets cat potty on it."

"*Passiflora* is a passion flower vine," I explained.

"I see," Ms. Jenkinson answered.

"Daddy? Can I go potty please?"

"Of course, sweetheart," Ms. Jenkinson said. "Let me take you."

"No, no, you don't need to do that," I said.

"It's really no bother, Mr. Menner."

"No, no, I mean I want to show you she can do it on her own. Violet's been going potty by herself for two months now. She still has some problems pooping, but she can potty now all by herself."

Finally, a raise of the eyebrow. "I have some handicaps as a stay-at-home dad," I said. "Let me explain."

As Violet skipped down the hallway, I recalled for Ms. Jenkinson the time I took her to see *Sesame Street on Ice* at the War Memorial downtown. Jo was out of town, on business in Nashville. We both had to pee at intermission, and I let her go first. She skipped into the large bathroom by herself and I posted guard outside the door as I always do. Men's bathrooms are no place for a little girl. Men's bathrooms stink. The toilets and floor are speckled with pee from a thousand bladders, and I don't like the idea of my fresh, pink little girl in there with all that pendulous man-flesh and hairy thighs and crushed cigarettes and gobs of spit on the floor.

The more difficult side of this is when I have to go to the bathroom. When I can hold it no longer, I make Violet stand at the entrance to the men's room and sing. It doesn't matter what she sings as long as she sings, and if the notes disappear I know she's been carried away.

At the War Memorial, I was halfway through urinating when the out-of-tune strains of the *Sesame Street* theme song abruptly stopped. In midstream, I stopped and sprinted to the entrance, stuffing myself back inside my zipper along the way. A long archipelago of dark pee stains trailed all the way down my blue jeans.

I bolted from the entrance. A woman was holding Violet's hand.

"Is this your child?" she asked.

"Violet! I told you never to stop singing when I'm in the bathroom."

"Daddy, this lady talks to me."

"Never, never, never stop singing! It's how I know nothing's happened to you."

"Do you always leave her alone in public places like this?" the woman asked.

"And what would you suggest?"

"Finding a woman to help you. I would have helped if you asked."

"And I don't know you from the Evil Queen. You're asking me to let a stranger take my daughter into a room, out of my vision."

"But what if something should happen out here?" she asked.

"Look at my situation here, I don't have a choice."

"I just don't think it's right," she said. "I'm sorry for butting in, but it takes a village to raise a child."

"And a meddlesome woman to ruin my afternoon. Thank you for making me piss my pants." She clicked away in her leather flats and Talbots Tahitian-print skirt, the same one I'd bought Jo as a celebration for making budget the previous year.

This anecdote managed to pull a smile from Ms. Jenkinson as we watched the reappearance of Violet, who wore orange tights that disappeared beneath a purple skirt with pink hibiscus blooms and a red-and-white-striped Hanna Andersen turtleneck.

"You certainly are colorful, Violet," Ms. Jenkinson said. "I like to dress like a parade," she said.

From the get-go, Jo and I had refused to dress Violet in pink clothes. Actually it was more my idea than hers. I do not understand everyone's obsession with people knowing the proper gender of their child. I dress Violet in whatever I buy at Target or get as gifts, and I let her pick out her own clothes. I think it fosters independent thinking and builds the foundation for a strong sense of style. On some days she emerges from her room with striped tights, fuchsia pumps from the dress-up box, Thomas the Tank Engine sweat shirt and a flowered skirt two sizes too short. Still, recently she has developed a preference for pink. This means I have two, sometimes three red loads of laundry per week.

"I'm trying to foster creativity and a strong sense of individuality," I explained.

Ms. Jenkinson shrank down to a squat then took Violet's hands into hers. "Would you like to come to school here, honey?" Violet nodded.

"I thought there was a waiting list," I said.

She returned to her feet. "Evidently you haven't spoken with your wife since yesterday."

"It happens sometimes," I said.

"I'm sure her job is unbelievably consuming. You must be very proud of her, being a gender pioneer in such a male-dominant industry."

It was my turn to nod as she continued.

"She called me yesterday with questions about the

school, and I assured her a spot. She's promised the school
a personal tour of the hospital. Isn't that wonderful?"

My internal reaction was as complex as Thai food, simultaneously spicy and sour and sweet. I was relieved to
get Violet into the school and might not have done so without Jo's call, but I felt coddled, even worse, belittled, like a
boy whose controlling father takes over the remote control
of the toy train.

We left the school and went shopping. It doesn't matter
what I buy—a book, a new bowl at Williams-Sonoma, a
rug or garden rake—purchasing something feeds me, fills
me up in some strange but insignificant way, like water
being poured into a glass, transparent and fleeting but oc-
cupying space nonetheless.

Still, there's this awful cycle: I buy things to make myself feel better, and then I feel guilty about spending
money because I don't earn any, so then I remember how
unfulfilled and unproductive I feel, which makes me depressed, which sends me back to the mall.

Most often I buy things for the house, and it's because I've become obsessed with every visual detail of my
home. This is more than a nesting instinct or boredom. I
think what we have here is a control issue, a delusion of
grandeur. Stay-at-home moms spend so much time within
the walls that they become kingdoms—growing grander
and larger in our minds as our real world shrinks—and we
are queen. And we take things very seriously in the kingdom, and we can do anything we want, just like teenagers

given free rein for decorating their bedroooms, a big deal to them, a speck of dust to the rest of the world.

In our homes we are omniscient experts. We can manipulate our spouses' surroundings in any way we choose— Yes, I do control something around here!—which renders us powerful and them powerless: *Honey, where did you move my underwear drawer? This is new shampoo, right? Why did we paint the fireplace?* Oh, here, let me help you, I'm in charge here, I can do this. I know what's going on even if you're helpless. You do need me—see?

I'd decided that the door to the back deck needed a new throw rug. I was thinking something deep and rich and Persian-like to counteract the light, neutral gray of the kitchen. We drove to RugWorld on Henrietta Road, a place so huge they organize the inventory by continent. Violet calls it "Aladdin's house," and she loves it. RugWorld is a textile labyrinth, random row after row of rugs hanging from the ceiling. It reminds me of the streets of Casablanca or Venice, dark and narrow with high walls closing in on the sides. At RugWorld, we are rats in a maze.

Violet likes leafing through the hanging rugs as if they were pages in a huge book. We also play what I call "Around the World." On our way from, say Morocco to China, I run, pushing her in the stroller through the fuzzy colorful walls.

During this trip, I found and bought a small kilim rug with rusts and greens that leaned toward olives and army-truck green. As we walked out of the store, I looked across the parking lot and noticed a new minimalist furniture dealer. Just one quick look, I told myself. Yet the second I wheeled into the store Violet began protesting.

"No, Daddy. I don't want to be here."

I don't know what it was—the gargoyle in the window, the swarthy, bearded man we passed walking inside—but Violet experienced a sudden, inexplicable need to flee. She erupted, tears and screams spewed forth, and began bucking up against the belt of her stroller with the intensity I remembered from *The Exorcist*, when Linda Blair pulls against the bonds that tie her to the bed.

"No! Nooooooooooooooo!" Violet screamed. "No, No, No, No! Stop, Stop!"

"Violet!" I yelled, crouching down on my haunches. Had she lost sight of me? Did she think I was gone? "This is unacceptable behavior! Unacceptable!"

"Stop! Stop! No, No, Noooooo!" She leaned back in the stroller, arching upward against the restraint, taut, like a bow just before release of the arrow. This is what it looked like: It looked like someone—me—had swiped this little girl from her mother's side in RugWorld, crammed her into a stroller and was preparing to cart her off to some unremarkable, inner-city, clapboard-style home where I would molest then kill and bury her beneath the porch.

I started pushing the stroller back to the car, acutely aware of the stares of passersby, most of them female. She never let up, screaming the entire way, writhing against the restraint. I was certain my credibility, my identity as her bona fide father, was contained solely in the stroller, my only visible icon of fatherhood. If I'd had to hold Violet in my arms, someone certainly would have stopped me.

I had to be careful. I could not rush or it would look as if I were fleeing. When someone would look at me I would shake my head, slightly roll my eyes in a weary way that said, "Okay, this again? Parenthood is absolute hell, don't you agree?"

All the way across the parking lot, she screamed.

"Noooooooooooo!"

All the way home, pushing up against the chest restraint in her car seat—"No, no, no, no!"—crying nonstop, her face pink-red as Spam. I drove, continually glancing at her in the rearview mirror, watching for clues. I know her moods and hot buttons. I take pride in anticipating and stifling her cries even before they materialize. My strong point in parenting and household management is preventive maintenance, anticipating any sounds or actions of discordance whether they come from metal or wire or plastic or human flesh, but what the hell was this outburst about?

When we pulled into the garage, Violet abruptly cut off the sobs, took a few deep, quivery breaths then fell into a sleep that would last five hours.

I went inside, put her to bed then called Jo, whom I pulled out of a meeting. I'm not certain why I called, I just knew I had to tell someone about this. When there is no adult in your presence for hours and days at a time, you tend to doubt and second-guess your reactions. You need a witness, for validation, for proof that whatever happened actually happened. Otherwise, you wonder all day long: Was it paranoia? Exaggeration? A lie? This happens almost daily. This is why you call another mother when something happens, good or bad, because you have to tell *someone*, even if they disagree with you, and this makes your reaction *real*. If you're very persuasive, you can get them to agree that your reaction was the right one even if it wasn't. Marilyn is good for this, a loyal friend who always agrees. It is times like this that I miss my mother.

To Jo's credit, she listened for a few minutes before shutting me off.

"Lincoln, I've got people in here. Is she okay or is she sick?"

"She's fine. She's sleeping," I replied.

"Can we talk about this when I get home?" she asked.

"Yeah, we will," I said. "And I want to talk about you calling the Montessori headmistress."

"I thought you'd be happy."

"You emasculated me, Jo! You think that's going to make me happy?"

"How do you emasculate a mom?" she asked. I could picture her smiling.

"Very funny, ha, ha, ha, I'm pissing my pants here laughing."

"I'm sorry. I used to be able to make you laugh, Lincoln."

"I don't have many spheres of influence left, Jo, and

you're treading on my sphere of influence. Violet is my sphere of influence."

"Violet is *our* daughter, Linc."

"Why are you always so combative with me?"

"Because you won't put down your gun. Jesus, Lincoln, you've become a soldier defending turf. Remember what I told you the other day about Patty?"

Despite my constant pleas for the contrary, Patty had not been running the kitchen rags through an extra rinse cycle. When I complained to Jo that evening, she took my hand and led me to the couch, like a mother leading a child, then sat down beside me. "Are you open to a mirror moment?" she asked. In our first year of marriage, Jo and I had agreed that a good spouse acts as personal shrink, and that no matter how painful it might be, it was that person's job to hold up a mirror to the other when he or she exhibited some personality trait or behavior that needed to be brought to light, all done in the most dignity-preserving way possible. I nodded.

"What need does Patty fill for you?" she asked.

"None. Nada. . . . Okay, she makes it possible for me to leave the house without Violet, but I could get one of the girls to do that."

"Do you expect the best from her?"

"Are you kidding?"

"Do you want her to disappoint you?"

"Where are you going with this?"

"I know you're not real high on yourself right now."

"And . . ."

"And, in the Kingdom of Lincoln that you've created here at home, she is the unenlightened, bumbling underclass. You've got Kaiser blood, Lincoln. You have to be in charge of something."

"And you think I need a fuckup like Patty around so I can feel better about myself?"

Jo stood up from the table, walked over to me, reached down and cupped my face in her hands. "You're a wonderful mother, Lincoln. I've never seen better, but you need to move on. This job is not you. Your lack of satisfaction with life is creating excruciating guilt in me."

I let Jo return to her meeting, hung up and turned on Nickelodeon. *Bewitched* was on. Mrs. Kravitz was complaining to her husband about Samantha again. I'd lately been seeing Mrs. Kravitz through new eyes. She would turn on her mouth like a faucet, and the sentences would gush out, nonstop, filling the room until her husband had no choice but to leave or drown in her words. He almost always leaves the room when she starts talking, and part of me can't blame him. Her words are empty and sharp like used tin cans. Nonetheless, he needs to listen, needs to show that woman some respect. She's his wife, and the very least he can do is pretend to be interested in what comes from her mouth, her *brain*.

"Sit back down, bucko," I commanded him, out loud, as he started to stand up in preparation for a quick escape.

I love Play-Doh, always have. The salty smell and cool, clammy touch. The way you press and cut and shape it, and it stays that way, obedient, until you change it. As a parent, I recognize its worth as a multitask teaching tool.

"What color is this, Violet?" I asked.

"Blue."

"Good. Now, make me a rectangle. Can you make me a rectangle with the blue Play-Doh?"

"Yes."

Her face scrunched in serious concentration, she took the rolling pin from my hand and pushed out a glob of blue. Then, with the yellow, plastic knife she cut out a crude rectangle, about the size of a Matchbox car. When engaged in a task, Violet has the same serious look of concentration as me, pinched, chin-to-the-wind with blinders on. Sometimes I worry that I'm making her too serious, too conscious of success and failure and completion. I've got to mellow out a little, I know. Childhood should not be so goal-oriented; it should be a sweet period of floating in the air, dipping down to earth for kisses and a quick hot dog and a good night's dreaming. But I have a job to do, and it is to develop my daughter's skills and intellect and emotions. My mother says I'm too intense, that I worry too much about parenting. "Relax and enjoy your daughter," she told me.

This grand advice from the woman who relaxed too much. Carol Menner was a lousy domestic manager, often gone from the house. Having given up a graphics design career when she married, she undertook huge art projects for people in town—painting murals, constructing mascot costumes for high schools—and I taught myself how to make grilled tuna sandwiches and Hamburger Helper for the three of us.

By the time I was in middle school, I was aiding in her struggle to keep my orderly father happy. ("What the hell do you do all day, Carol?") I painted porch steps and scoured the moldy lines of grout in the bottom of the shower. I would make their bed if it wasn't done by five o'clock. Mom would do the wash, but it was I who would chip away at the Matterhorn of clothes on the bed every day after school, sometimes folding for an hour at a time. She also taught me to iron my dad's shirts and how to make an omelet, all of which I didn't mind doing because it was better than witnessing the clash between Mr. Now and Mrs. Mañana. I learned long ago how to find pleasure in a taut sheet and stainless-steel shine.

The phone rang. I stood to answer it, setting a ball of blue Play-Doh on the table.

"Okay, Violet, that's good, honey, that's good. Now, make me another rectangle. . . . Good. Now look at what you have. One plus one equals two."

"Blue!" she said.

"Yes, blue rhymes with two. But how many rectangles do you have there? Two, right?"

It was Nan Phipps on the phone. I'd expressed a desire at the lunch to lose the gut, and she was calling to ask if I wanted to join her and a friend for early-morning walks. This was great news, considering that I thought I'd scared them all out of my life forever during that lunch.

"I'd like to but I can't," I said. "Jo usually leaves at six."

"And Jim leaves at a quarter till, so we're talking really early. Is five-fifteen okay?"

"Great. I need this. You don't know how much I need this."

"You want to start tomorrow?"

"Absolutely."

Since being at home I have learned to love mornings, the only predictable island of calmness and solitude in my day, and I have to grab it and run. My day is a ball at the top of a gradual incline. It rolls along slowly at first but gains momentum in its journey, reaching peak speed at midafternoon when preparation of dinner collides with telemarketers and all the other chores I didn't finish that morning.

My favorite thing to do in this precious chunk of time is to read the newspaper in the bathtub. Bathing is a guilt-free activity. Though something always is screaming to be filled or delivered or fixed, everyone's got to take time out to clean, and personal hygiene is a private matter. No kids allowed. Taking baths and eating combine sensual pampering with necessary tasks. Bathing is clever multitasking, especially when you add a magazine, a bowl of cherries, a cup of coffee.

"Come on, Violet," I said. "Please put the lid back on the Play-Doh. Let's go see what Patty's made you to eat."

I had told Patty that Violet needed to have some creamed spinach for lunch, yet when I came downstairs I smelled potatoes frying on the stove.

"Potatoes are vegetables," she said.

"Potatoes are a starch."

Patty crinkled her nose. "No kid wants to eat that." She motioned with her pointy chin to the spinach on the counter. "Eeesh! You eat it!"

I walked over, picked up the untouched spinach and put it in the sink. "I'm sick of you not doing as I say."

"What do you mean?"

"Don't treat me like a stupid man, Patty. I'm not oblivious. Let me tell you a secret here. The reason men are so oblivious to the details of the workings of a house is because they choose to be. Ignorance buys them leisure time. But this is my job, and I know everything—everything—that happens inside these walls."

"Why do you keep picking on me?"

"Because you lie to me, that's why, and you don't do as I say. And I constantly have to baby-sit you."

I was forcing her to the end of the plank, like Captain Hook at the close of *Peter Pan*. The tick-tock of the hungry alligator below. Jump, Patty. Jump.

Date: Thurs. 23 Jan.
From: BigEasyPack-n-send@infi.net
To: LincolnM@aol.com
How is work going? The cacti? And speaking of pricks: I need to apologize to you for something your father and I did to you years ago: YOUR NAME. Your father wanted a name of greatness, one that you could fill in your climb to perfection, and in his little mind the Lincoln Continental is the finest car in the world. I should have stood up to him. I just wasn't into standing up to anyone back then. Mothers from my era just don't do that. (I guess I should put that in past tense, no?) They make a bad life decision then suck it up and stay in it because they have children, and those children, after all, are their first responsibility. The difference between your generation and mine is that mine recognizes the need for personal sacrifice in a society; sacrifice is the glue that holds civilization together. But all wells run dry, and I've pulled up my last bucket of sacrifice. Your generation, on the other hand, thinks sacrifice is using French's because it's the only mustard in the restaurant. Enough preaching. . . . . I always wanted to come to New Orleans, and here I am. Your father hasn't canceled the credit cards on me yet. . . . maybe he hasn't thought of it. I've been sending him e-mails with no response. Why hasn't he called the police? I told him I'm okay and not to worry, that I just needed to get away and that I might possibly decide to come back. Kiss Violet for me. Jo, too.

Perhaps they did it to make me feel at ease, but the first week of walks with the women were filled mainly with their questions pertaining to food and landscaping. Nan Phipps was in the process of redesigning her backyard and wanted to know the hardiness of various waxy, evergreen hedges. Joanne Thomasen, a take-out gourmand who'd been re-born by her cooking classes at the Williams-Sonoma at Seneca Hills Mall, sought knowledge on cuts of beef and how they held up to slow roasting.

They showered me with flattery for household success and, having spent eight months in this compliment-free zone called home, I lapped it up. More than anything, they wanted to know how I could drop so easily into their world and thrive like basil in full sun. I explained how running a house is very similar to landscaping. It is big-picture think-ing, keeping your eye on everything at once, alert to pests and problems that could endanger or hinder overall suc-cess. In good landscaping, as in good housekeeping, there is no such thing as universal broadcast. Some plants and situations need extra fertilizer, some require more lime in the soil or constant spraying for mealy bugs. Some species thrive while others wither because it's in their nature to do so.

"I do wish my mom would come home, though," I said. "She's been gone at the time I've needed her most. I'm ac-tually a little pissed off at her right now."

"Why?" Nan asked. I'd already given them the history of Carol Menner's Odyssey. Rarely a walk would pass when we did not discuss her.

"She's being incredibly self-indulgent," I said. "And irresponsible."

"She deserves it!" Joanne said, exaggeratingly pumping her arms as I'd shown her to achieve maximum aerobic gain. "She's raised her kids, pampered her husband. She's just taking the vacation that's due."

"Don't you worry about her?" Nan asked.

Immediately I thought of Mom's car. When leaving town to visit us, she would pack not one but three huge coolers, one up front with sandwiches and grapes and two others in the backseat filled with things like pomegranates, kalamata olives, fresh jalapeños, fat-free hot dogs and bottles of Perrier that clinked over bumps. She squirreled away dental floss, books on tape and her asthma ventilators into every crevice and dark spot. One time, when I went out to the car to get her book, I saw on top of a folded easel and inflatable raft a wire basket filled with shampoo, paints and brushes, a pair of vice grips, children's books, heads of dirty, home-grown garlic, an extra pair of shoes, canned chicken noodle soup and three or four rain ponchos. I knew that in order to survive all my mom needed was $200 and a trip to Target, and she'd be just fine for months.

"She's Wandering Jew," I said to the women as we topped the hill at Pheasant Hollow Drive, near the house of the bold man who, despite all neighborhood bickering, covered his half-million-dollar house at Christmastime in those big knobby colored bulbs instead of the suburban-sanctioned tiny white lights that make each bush innocuously twinkle like a miniature milky way.

"Wandering Jew?" Nan asked.

"That purple variegated ground cover with the tiny pink flowers."

"I don't know it."

"It'll grow anywhere. You rip it from the ground, toss it over your shoulder and in a week you find twenty new plants that have taken root."

"I can't believe your dad hasn't called the police," Joanne said. "Roger would have me dragged back home in a day."

"Who's taking care of him?" Nan asked.

"Dairy Queen," I said. "He orders the same double-cheese hamburger and fries every night."

"Isn't he mad at her?" Nan asked.

"I think he's just cutting her some slack because he feels guilty."

"About what?" Joanne asked.

"About all those things that working spouses need to feel guilty about."

Their laughter pierced the darkness of Hunter's Glen Road, where the houses all in a line reminded me of the little girls sleeping in the rows of beds in Madeline's school, all covered in vines. In the next half hour, each of these houses would begin to wake up, a light in the window flicking on like the opening of an eye. For some of these families, those with a mother who worked outside the home, the day would begin with a jolt. There would be no time for that sweet crawl from sleep into consciousness. For them, waking up was like jumping onto an already spinning treadmill. Maybe, if they could hop on and keep their balance, they might be able to grab a donut in one hand, a briefcase or homework papers in the other, then begin a mad run into a noisy, hungry and dizzying world. I spot these moms at Wegmans in the late afternoon. Still dressed for work, their morning makeup long since evaporated, they pull frozen Tater Tots and Ragú spaghetti sauce and Caesar salad in a bag from their carts and onto the whining conveyor belt, all the time their brows furrowed in a contemplation of logistics: How and when will I get the garbage disposal fixed or the extra socks cleaned for the next morning's football practice?

I am spoiled, I know this. I have grown accustomed to the luxury of plucking Violet out of bed, grabbing a book and rocking and reading with her in her room, maybe for half an hour. We can make banana pancakes if we want to. We don't even have to get out of our jammies. Some days we never do.

The perennial growers' convention was being held in Buffalo, just sixty miles away. Without telling me, Jo had spotted the news in the *Democrat and Chronicle* and called and made reservations for me.

"You need to go to this, Lincoln. You haven't missed this convention for years."

"But I'm not working."

"But you will be. You need to go. This will be good for you."

"It's too far away," I said, watching her pull on pantyhose.

Buy more hose.

Birthday card for Jo's mother.

Happy birthday to you . . . you live in a zoo.

Get Violet out of the house on more field trips. Enrich her!

Enriched flour. Why do they add vitamins?

"It's one day, Lincoln. I even called Anna to baby-sit."

"For all day? I can't trust anybody all day with Violet. I can't do that, Jo. Violet's too young. There are just too many details about her daily routine. I'm the only one who understands."

"She's not on life-support, Lincoln."

"You just don't understand."

She walked up, put her open hands on my cheeks and squeezed my head with the same force you use to determine if a pineapple is ripe. "Stop . . . being . . . so . . . controlling! Loosen your grip a little. You're strangling yourself."

I walked out to the kitchen to get a drink of water. I looked up at my passion flower vine, which had since tired of the dining room and crept into the kitchen, and noticed it had dipped down from the ceiling, reached for and crawled onto the top edge of a cabinet door. The tiny green tendril reminded me of an arm jutting out of the water, pulling itself onto a life raft. Mom.

I fished for my tape measure in the junk drawer by the telephone. In just four more feet, the plant, if I was accurately predicting the path, would reach the two-story foyer. In all, it was forty-one feet long. *Passiflora* watches me in the kitchen as I work. Sometimes I'll say something to it when I'm alone: Hey, little guy. You go, girl. Male or female, I'm not sure. Which gender better fits this restless, graceful personality that thrives while searching for something better?

"What time is Anna coming?" I yelled to Jo in the bedroom.

"Eight."

"What time does it start?"

"Ten."

Quickly, I sat down to type out directions:

Anna: I will be at the horticulture show at the convention center in Buffalo (2455 Third Street) all day long. My cell phone, which will be on my belt loop: 555-6765. Jo's number at work: 555-5543. Poison Control: 555-7884. Police and Ambulance: 911. Tell dispatcher our house is fourth in from Quail Run Road, left-hand side.

8 A.M. to 9 A.M.: Violet usually eats during this time. Make sure you give her cereal, about one cup, with your choice of fresh berries AND banana. Orange juice is a must. If she doesn't drink it during breakfast, she will drink it during Barney, which begins at 9 A.M. on PBS, channel 35. Whatever you do, don't make her eat more than she wants. If she says she's full she means it. I don't want to give her any hang-ups about food.

9 A.M. to 11 A.M.: Violet enjoys playing on the swing set outside. If it's cool out make sure she wears her pink jacket, flannel-lined, that's hanging in the hall closet. Be sure to snap top snap in addition to zipping all the way up. Encourage her to swing by herself. Work with her on this. She seems to have problems coordinating the foot action of the pumping motion with leaning back.

If she wants to stay outside, perhaps you can draw on the driveway with the sidewalk chalk, located on floor beside steps that lead into house from garage. Show how you can mix colors to make new colors.

11 A.M. to noon: If she starts to get fussy it means she's hungry. I've left for her some precooked tortellinis. Be sure to heat these in the microwave then toss with olive oil and garlic salt. I've also cut up cantaloupe (see top shelf behind berries). Please clean up kitchen when you're finished. Do NOT put any wooden spoons in the dishwasher as this dries them out. And please do not cut anything directly on the Corian.

Noon to 1 P.M.: If it's too cool to play outside for long you might want to play a video. You also might want to get the art-supply box and paint on the kitchen floor, underneath the plastic tablecloth I keep in the drawer under the stove. I've been using watercolors to show Violet how unpredictable and untamable water can be, but you can use the acrylics if you wish. When washing the brushes, do not bend bristles backward as this ruins the shape of the brush.

Also, please make sure the cat's bowl on the back deck still has food in it. I've been having trouble with a stray eating it all. If it's empty, please add one cup of Meow Mix (on floor beside washer) to the bowl.

1 P.M. to 3 P.M.: You might want to go to the park. You can walk if you like, but it takes too long because Violet dawdles at every crack in the sidewalk. At the playground, I encourage her to take brave moves, like the monkey bars and the slide that winds like a corkscrew. If you stay home, you can play some games, which I keep in the armoire next to the fireplace. Violet loves to play Concentration, the game in which you turn all the cards upside down and try to find matching pairs. She's getting good at this, but whatever you do, do not LET her win; play your best. If she wins, great. If not, then that, too, is an important lesson, and she will try harder next time.

Also, please bring mail in from mailbox and set it on my desk in the kitchen.

3 P.M. to 5 P.M.: In the refrigerator, second shelf from bottom, I've left a white-with-blue-stripes glass roasting pan filled with chicken, root vegetables and various

Mediterranean spices. At 5 P.M., please put it in the oven for an hour. I should be home by the time it's ready. If I don't get back in time, turn off oven and keep the lid on.

Violet may need a nap during this time. If her eyes seem heavy and if she seems grouchy, then have her lie down with the binky and blue blanket with bunnies on it. Please remember that she is allowed the binky only while in bed.

Also: During the day, please read a minimum of three books to Violet.

Please remember, Anna, that if you have questions about absolutely anything, just call me. I'd rather be bothered than to have something go wrong.

Thanks. I'm sure you'll do fine. Linc.

Marilyn called and asked me to come over and poke through the garage because she had heard a noise. Steven was hunting in the Boundary Waters of Minnesota, and between work and play he'd been gone most of the month, which meant Marilyn and I had been cooking lunch together three or four times a week.

I zipped Violet into her parka and mittens, put on my duck boots and trudged through the fresh snow over to her house.

The garage door was open so Violet and I walked inside. It was she who found them. "Kitties, Daddy! Look at the kitties! Oh, oh, oh, kitties!"

They couldn't have been more than a week old, their eyes still shut. I took off my stocking cap and lay the kittens inside, then knocked on the door. No answer. I knocked again, knowing very well she was inside. We trudged around the house, to the front door, which is flanked by windows that run from door top to bottom, and rang the bell. Finally, Marilyn appeared, saw it was us and opened the door.

"Please tell me that was you knocking in the garage."

"It was me."

She sighed and patted her chest in a be-still-my-heart manner. "I was so scared. Oh, Linc, what would I have done if you weren't here?"

"Probably fed these guys some milk," I said, showing her my hat of wriggling white-and-gray fur. "Where's the mom?"

"How should I know?"

"You want them?"

"Steven hates cats."

"Do you mind if I take them home?"

She shook her head.

"Call me if you see the mom," I said, "but I think something's happened to her."

"Can you come in for a while?" she asked.

"I'm in the middle of making pasta. You wanna come over later and have some? Early dinner?"

"Six-ish?"

"Okay."

By the end of the afternoon, it was evident something had happened to the mother. Violet and I took the kittens to Dr. Chu, the vet who had lanced a growth on Tillie's hind quarter right after we moved to Rochester.

"These cats, you must teach them to urinate," he said to us in the examination room.

"I thought they buried their business by instinct," I said.

"No, no. You must teach them *how* to pee. The mother licks the genitals to stimulate urine flow, and this is how he learns."

"Oh. great. And I'm supposed to do what?"

"Here. I show you."

Dr. Chu snapped on a rubber glove then carried one of the cats over to the sink. "Both of them, they are boys," he said. With his index finger, he rubbed in a clockwise motion on the kitty's furry balls, both of them together no bigger than a dime. Within five seconds, it loudly mewed then released a salty-smelling yellow stream of urine.

"Kitty's going pee-pee!" Violet squealed, clapping her hands.

"How long will I have to do that?" I asked.

"Not long. Maybe ten days, maybe two weeks."

"Oh, maaaaaan." I was not pleased. Now I had to deal with the digestive products of two more creatures. "Can I buy some of those gloves from you?" I asked.

With tiny baby bottles borrowed from Violet's doll, I fed the cats every two to three hours. They stopped crying only if I held them. I resorted to carrying them in a hammock fashioned from a large dish towel tied to the belt loops of my jeans. It didn't matter how much I moved around, they always seemed happier if they were up against my body.

As planned, Marilyn and the kids came over for dinner. We were breading veal for saltimbocca when both cats woke up and stretched their heads over the edge of the hammock, which hung right at my crotch line.

"You're a mama kangaroo," Marilyn said. She dipped down to her knees and powdered one of the cat's noses with flour. I looked down from my veal when I noticed that the laughter had run out but she hadn't returned to her feet. Her smile now melted into seriousness, Marilyn looked up at me, straight into my eyes then back down at my hammock. She hesitated a moment then reached inside, her fingers fumbling and rubbing against me—I felt myself getting hard—until she finally pulled out two hungry kittens.

She stood up and looked at me, saying nothing, holding the cats around the bellies with their legs dangling, as if they were creatures of cuisine we'd just bought at market.

"Is something wrong?" I asked, taking them from her.

"I don't understand you, Linc."

"What do you mean?"

She walked over to the sink and started washing the flour from her hands. "Never mind," she said. "Let's fry the meat."

Of course I knew what she meant; she had lingered for too long on her knees, and the retrieval of the cats was one second short of fondling. I needed more sex, I knew this. My problem with Jo has been compatibility—our schedules are not sexually compatible. It would be so easy to have an affair, even just one afternoon. Jo would never know. A Teletubbies show lasts thirty minutes, and that's all the time we would need in my office behind a locked door. Marilyn always seems to run hot, a radiator turned on low. I can feel the heat emanating from her body whenever I stand behind her at the sink or stove. On more than one occasion I'd thought of the food-and-sex-frenzy scenes from the movie *9¹/₂ Weeks,* and I wondered what it would be like to end up on the floor, bodies slipping against each other as we feverishly grabbed at arms, legs, breasts, neck, our skin slathered in olive oil or chocolate sauce.

Short-term ecstasy, however, would spell long-term hell. I could not live with myself, me, Linc Menner, son of the World's Most Loyal Man. I did not desire more love in my life, or another person clinging to me for reasons of need.

The Pittsford Village Hall is a contemporary German artist dressed in his grandma's clothes. Designers decided not to touch the eighteenth-century, granite and sandstone exterior of the old church it occupies, yet inside there are soaring ceilings and gray minimalist work cubicles and Mondrian-ish paintings on the walls and reflective halogen lighting. I like this don't-judge-a-book-by-its-cover juxtaposition. I like the marriage of traditional and unpredictable.

Just as the girls had intimated to me on one of our walks, it is the stay-at-home moms who have the time, and therefore the responsibility, to preserve the ideals and expectations and standards of our culture. Therefore, I decided to visit the village hall after getting a disturbing letter from the village administrator in my mailbox: *Because the village recycling program is not profitable, we will scale back our operations and collect recyclables every two weeks instead of every week.*

I introduced myself to a man named Phil, the assistant public works director who wore a Polo oxford-cloth shirt, creased pants, black Italian loafers and a tie with the perfect dimple found on men in financial districts.

"You're the man who wanted us to throw the Christmas trees in Raspberry Lake, aren't you?" he asked. I had called them around New Year's after reading research in a horticulture trade pub that said the trees make ideal spawning grounds for fish.

"That's me," I replied. "I'm also the one who's been trying to get you to set up a community compost pile. I think I talked to you, didn't I?"

"Yeah."

"Any progress?"

"No."

We spoke in the main lobby, standing, separated by the counter. Violet busied herself with paper dolls on the floor by the front door. They were dolls of famous role-model women—Margaret Mead, Eleanor Roosevelt and others— yet Violet was dressing them in elaborate gowns borrowed from her Cinderella paper doll set she'd got from Jo's aunt for her birthday. By now I'd conceded to Violet in the Battle of Barbie, my effort to stress to her that physical beauty should pale in comparison to character, that sequins and ruby lips and golden locks are unnecessary, if not undesirable, traits. Yet I'd learned, by watching Violet and her friends, that little girls like beautiful things, and I cannot expect to change that, just as I cannot expect to satisfyingly lose myself in motherhood. I am impatient and tunnel-minded, incapable of letting children occupy more than 20 percent of my pantry of emotions. Conversely, a mother and her child remind me of a grafting of two fruit trees, genes and tissue infused into one another until there is one body, and over time neither can distinguish one from the other, they become a new creation, sacrificing personal identity to create anew. Though I want to feel this way I cannot. Instead, I compartmentalize. I am solely a care provider, nothing more, no matter how many cheese sticks I unwrap and hours of make-believe I play. I love Violet. She is my job, and I do my job very well.

The man kept looking at Violet as I tried to educate him about recycling, stressing that it was an investment for the future and that we shouldn't expect to make any money from it.

"Yeah well thanks for your input," he said when I finally stopped.

"You're not even listening to me, are you?" I asked.

"No offense, but do you know how busy we'd be if we listened to everyone who called in with some idea?"

"Did it ever dawn on you that some of them might be good ideas?"

He leaned forward, onto the counter, resting on his elbows.

"Listen, buddy, between you and me, most of what we get is from a bunch of ladies out there who really like their white wine and have too much time on their hands. The

Pittsford princesses, know what I mean? I had someone call one day to complain about one of my guys because he was mowing the cemetery without a shirt on. That's the crap I have to put up with."

I should have said something, but it caught me by surprise. It had been so long since another guy spoke to me like this, including me in the Man Club, where bitch-bashing is acceptable as humor and therapy and a camaraderie-builder.

"So today is dad's day to baby-sit, huh?" he asked.

"Actually, I'm home with her all the time. I'm the primary caregiver."

"No kidding?"

Whenever this dad-at-home topic comes up, this is the fork in the path of the conversation where the two genders take different paths. Women burst forth with a fountain of questions. Almost always, men drop it immediately. They ask nothing. They're mystified but not curious. That's all they want to know. They never ask me, "What's it like?" They never smile and say, "I wish I could do that." Men have women exactly where they want them.

I reached down to the floor to help Violet collect her paper dolls.

"I want to ask you something," he said.

I looked up. "Yeah?"

"You have a pretty good understanding of plants. What did you do when you used to work?"

Give it up, Lincoln, I said to myself. Don't correct him.

Shove the soapbox back under the bed and answer the man's question.

"I'm a landscape architect."

"Commercial or residential?"

"Both. I've done projects as big as the Los Angeles Museum of Art."

"No kidding? . . . Did you know the village is looking for a full-time horticulturist?"

I stood up, paper dolls in hand. "Yeah? What's the job description like?"

"Like being aesthetics czar for Pittsford, to keep the village looking pretty and the subjects happy, which is not an easy task. All parks, all roadways, everything that's planted. Staff of eight or nine, I can't remember."

"That sounds like a great job," I said.

"California, huh?"

"California."

"You should apply."

"I should apply," I said, nodding.

On the way home I could not help but notice every plant in the medians on Main Street and in the rights-of-way of Washington Road. It could look so much better! Replace the dull-green junipers with fuchsia-blooming rhododendron. Control the weeds with another two inches of cypress mulch. And in front of city hall, planters bursting with something of white blooms to denote openness and purity and faith in public government.

Violet had reached for my hand as we walked down the

sidewalk of Washington Road. We would stop at Schoen Place, down on the Erie Canal, and feed the ducks the crusts I'd crammed into my back pocket, back there with the earring I'd found under the sofa and the invoice for the dry cleaning we would pick up tomorrow.

Violet squeezed my hand. I gently squeezed in reply: *Yes, yes, I'm here, sweetie, I'm here.*

"Watch it!" I snapped.

"What! What!" Patty barked, jumping back from the counter.

I'd been standing behind her, watching, because I knew she wouldn't exercise caution in opening and closing the cabinet that holds the drinking glasses. *Passiflora* had dipped down from the ceiling, into the path of the cabinet door and was in danger of being crushed.

"I asked you to watch out for the plant," I said.

"What else am I gonna do? I can't reach the frickin' thing."

"Then get the foot stool. Don't be so damned lazy."

"You've got a real weird thing for that plant. Who ever heard of letting a plant take over the house like some snake or something? It's weird, that's what it is."

Patty wore turquoise spandex stirrup pants that disap-peared beneath a black sweatshirt masquerading as a tunic, which had the phrase "Mall Princess" inscribed on the chest in glittery, pink letters. As a landscape architect I'd

learned long ago of the majority of Americans, Patty obviously included in this, who could not notice, let alone
understand, beauty until it had morphed from subtlety
into the flashy equivalent of a teal-green Camaro or two
dozen red roses, the sugared cereal of the flower world.

I knew she could not recognize and appreciate *passiflora*'s beauty in aggression, how the plant tirelessly births
tendril after tendril, reaching onward. Jo, too, had ques-
tioned my intentions with the plant, and I suppose I'd developed a feeling that by the time *passiflora*'s journey was
over, mine would be as well, each inch another mark on the
wall as I counted days past or future, I wasn't sure which.
And what was I counting? Days or years until full-time elementary school? Number of days left until no more pull-
ups at night? What end or beginning did I desire?

Patty lifted the tortellinis from the stove and walked
over to the sink to drain them.

"Don't forget the carrots," I said.

"I'm not gonna do that with those carrots. It's too
much work."

"She needs the beta carotene."

"She takes a vitamin."

"Yeah, but we seem to be running out every week because someone around here is eating the chewable Bugs
Bunnies like candy."

"What the frick? What are you looking at me for?"

"Why do you think?"

"I didn't do it."

"Whatever, Patty."

I retrieved the carrots from the freezer myself, then nuked a handful of the tiny orange cubes in a shallow bowl of water. Violet had been rebelling with the vegetables, a side-effect of the potty-training issue, I was certain, but she had to get her vitamins.

With a paring knife, I sliced a tiny incision into the first tortellini, then pushed the piece of carrot inside until it was swallowed and hidden by steaming pale-yellow cheese.

It is difficult, though not impossible, for me to relinquish all control of something. Yet when Violet's fourth birthday rolled around, and I was scurrying to throw a portfolio together for the Pittsford horticulturalist job, I bit at Jo's offer to organize and implement the party.

I had told my walking buddies that I was doubtful she would pull it off, and I made emergency plans, including a frozen TCBY cake stowed in the deep freezer in the garage. Jo had been shuttling back and forth to corporate headquarters in Nashville, and she was scheduled to be out of town the two days before the party.

Just as I was losing faith, I started getting signs that she was working the party long distance. Marilyn called to say Jo had issued verbal invites to the mothers of the neighborhood. A woman named Rebecca of Sunnydale Farm called to ask where she could park her horse trailer.

At eight A.M. on the day of the party, while Jo was still in Nashville, I answered the door to find David, a freelance display designer who, I later discovered, was the creator of the whacked-out window displays Jo and I frequently admired at the Canal Pharmacy in downtown Pittsford. I drank my coffee and watched him and his entourage let

loose with a flurry of crepe paper and aluminum Christmas-
tree icicles and blue cellophane, transforming the family
room into some artsy version of a fantasy-world ice cave.
The final touch was a huge chifforobe with the back panel
cut away, which they set in the foyer. Guests had to walk
through the piece of furniture to enter the wonderland.
Aha, I realized, *The Lion, the Witch and the Wardrobe*. I was
impressed. From Nashville, Jo had re-created the land of
Narnia in our living room.

In the next hour, a baker from Wegmans delivered
punch and the cakes and a platter of something baked and
white that looked like the Turkish Delight Edmund devours in the book. Soon after that, Rebecca and her horses
arrived, followed by the magician. The party was to begin
at three. Jo blew into the house at two-fifty, carrying a large
stuffed lion under her arm and a bag of blue paper plates
and cups.

"You are unbelievable, woman," I said. "This is way too
cool."

She stood back and surveyed the family room, her gaze
stopping at the hanging light from the ceiling, which had
been wrapped in blue cellophane to resemble a huge piece
of candy with twisties at each end. I had not seen this
sparkle and delight in her eyes for months. When her job
was easier—and I'm hoping we'll get there again some
day—Jo had pursued party planning with the polish of
Martha Stewart and the whimsy of Pee-Wee Herman. I remembered our party for the farewell episode of *M*A*S*H*
and how she borrowed those molded tin trays from the ele-

mentary school down the street and hired one of her Asian friends to dress up as Rosie the bar owner and serve Grape Nehis tainted with gin.

"It is wonderful, isn't it?" she said. "How long did it take them?"

"Three or four hours," I answered.

"It's fantastic. They even brought the Christmas-tree icicles like I asked."

Smiling, Jo bounced on her toes and made quick clicking sounds with her tongue. She seemed ready to burst, a child waiting in the entrance line at Disneyland. I felt a sudden, urgent need to connect with her.

"Come here," I said.

"What?"

I pointed to the spot on the floor in front of me.

"Yes?" she asked.

I kissed her, nestling her top lip, wet and moist like a piece of warm papaya, between the two of mine.

"You shaved," she said, bringing her hand to my face.

"Of course I shaved."

The doorbell rang, the door opened. "Hello?" Marilyn yelled. "Are we early? What the hell is this in the doorway?"

"Walk on through the wardrobe," Jo yelled.

I suddenly realized that although Marilyn and Jo had met each other, they remained strangers. Both women immediately took on that distant, icy politeness I see in first-time encounters between kids on the playground, just as they're starting to check each other out.

"We meet again," Jo said, thrusting out her hand. "Glad you could make it."

Again, the doorbell rang. Jo went to answer.

Marilyn scanned the room. "Wow," she said. "How long did it take you?"

"Not me. My wife the delegator extraordinaire."

"Really?"

"Yeah."

"That surprises me. This isn't the woman you've described to me."

"That's because you just get to hear all the bad stuff."

It was true that my relationship with Marilyn had toxic overtones, I could see this now. In these months of transition I had needed someone to validate my belief that life was unfair and unsavory. Considering this requirement, she'd been the best of friends.

Over the next two hours we played pin the tail on Aslan. We had a *Sesame Street* trivia contest, and winners earned a piece of Turkish delight. As I was spooning ice cream onto the blue plates, Jo walked over and stood beside Marilyn. Both of them watched me, arms folded, and I strained to listen. Their conversation had the crisp edge of a skate blade cutting across ice. I had not told Jo about the kitty incident. I didn't feel the need because intent on my part had been absent. My walking partners had been right when they said your spouse does not need to know everything, especially if it's something that will upset her, something over which she has no control. Still, I wondered if it was possible for Jo to know something had happened. Women are masters at absorbing and deciphering nuance, almost to the point of mind-reading. I wasn't there yet, but I was getting closer.

"He's a great guy, isn't he?" Jo said to her. Marilyn nodded. "I was wondering, Marilyn . . ."

"Yeah?"

"Would you mind watching Violet tonight? I need to inject some romance into my marriage and I actually have the evening free."

Whoa, I thought, impressive. A male dog urinating on its territory.

"I'd be happy to," Marilyn said. "I spend a lot of time with your daughter. Watching Violet is never a problem. Linc's done such a good job with her."

Zing! And the score was tied.

That night, we walked down to a new restaurant on Pittsford's Main Street, La Diablo, owned by a French-Mexican couple who had retired from teaching jobs at Monroe Community College.

I was eating my appetizer—foie gras seared in corn oil, drizzled with a smoky chipotle dressing and topped with crumbs of chèvre—when Jo brought up my mother.

"I logged on last night and read all the e-mails. I particularly was amused by the one from Sanibel Island."

It also was my favorite among the dispatches from Carol-in-Exile. She'd been out on a fishing boat in the Gulf when a fat, sunburned tourist from Indiana fell into the water as he stood on the edge of the bow, taking a leak. She was moved by the image of a ring buoy sailing through the air, slapping against the water. She wanted to jump in, swim over to the thing and grab it herself. Surely, someone would pull her back in, back to some place where people expected her return: *Oh, Carol, we missed you. We took you for granted. This is the least we can do for all the comforting and nurturing and saving you've done for us over the years.* Was Mom waiting for Dad to pull her back in? This was a test, I was fairly certain by now, but would Dad pass? Should I help him? Would that be considered helpful or traitorous? When the ride was over, the rope shortened, the water cleared from the eyes, whom did she want to find at the end?

"What has your dad been saying about all this?" she asked.

"Not much, really, you know how he is."

"I don't want to be like them, Lincoln. I worry that's what we're becoming."

"We're not that bad off, Jo. We're healing. You're settling into your job. I'm happier now. This move has been hell on us."

Jo stood up, walked over to my side of the table. She lay her chin on my shoulder, wrapped her arms around my chest, then squeezed. "I love you so much, Lincoln. Violet is the sweetest, smartest child in the world and it's all because of you."

I felt a flood of heat surge from my solar plexus, travel up my torso and into my neck and arms and fingers, making me feel like a greenhouse in late summer afternoon. My job at home would be so much easier if I had had a steady dose of this.

"You are happier, aren't you?" she said. "Half a day in Montessori has helped your mood immensely."

This reminded me that I'd forgotten to tell Jo about being on television the night before, when she was in Nashville, and I proceeded to tell her my embarrassing story. A film crew had visited Violet's preschool that day, hoping to get some footage for a story on the early spring we seemed to be having. I really hadn't spoken much with them directly, but they shot footage of me helping the kids rake the soil and pull dandelions and chickweed. The garden is my niche at the school. The headmistress evidently does not like me in the classroom with the other mothers. I feel like the janitor interloper in a movie, the scary disfigured man who always steps out from behind the door. Yet really the only thing that bothers me is how the other mother volunteers ignore me as they would their yard men or plumbers or deck builders. They are cordial, not inclusive. Actually, I like being invisible at Violet's school. It allows me to stand back and notice things I never could see up close. If I were down there on the floor with them all, I never would have discovered what I call The Dance of the Little Girls. The kids sit four to a rectangular table, two on each side. Usually they pair boys with boys and girls with girls. The boys rarely interact, except to push or jab or try to gross each other out. But the girls, as they sit throughout the morning, cutting or coloring or simply listening, weave and bend back and forth, leaning into each other's bubble of space. A head might touch a head, an arm might brush an arm, a leg might kiss a foot. They never consciously acknowledge the connection, but they do it again and again and again. It's beautiful to watch. It reminds me of seaweed plants slowly waving back and forth in the current on the ocean floor. In comparison, the boys seem so alone.

I listened and watched the television footage in horror. Most people say they don't like their voices on tape, that a camera or tape recorder distorts them somehow, but recorders actually are as accurate as mirrors. Everyone else's voice sounds normal on the tape. It's just that your ears hear your own voice differently. *This* is how you sound. And, gently guiding each child in a gardening task, I sounded like a gay sales clerk. Men speak from deep in the chest, pushing words out in a way that makes the throat, the entire upper torso vibrate like speakers with the bass turned on high. Women, on the other hand, seem to talk from somewhere higher, not from the chest but from the very top and back of the throat, somewhere back there in Tonsil Country. My man's voice had been sanded down into something as smooth and hairless as the inside of a woman's thigh. Did I talk this way all the time? Had Jo noticed? And what did she think? How could she be attracted to me when I talked like such a fem? And why did I talk like this? Was I remembering my own mother's voice? Or was there something about the female voice that works better on children, and I subconsciously discovered this and chose the voice as I would the proper tool for a fix-it job?

After watching the segment, I urgently needed for Jo to hear me talk. Talk like Linc The Man. I called the hospital, but she evidently was on the phone because I got her voice mail. In my deepest, most man-buzzing voice I asked if she could stop by Wegmans on the way home from work and buy a quart of milk.

Jo was laughing so hard at this point that she had to wipe her eyes. She breathed deeply to regain her breath and reached across the table for my hand. "I wondered what that message was about," she said. "You sounded like some little boy playing policeman. . . . Oh, Lincoln. You are so, so, so far from being a woman."

Thank God, I thought. And then a stranger reaction slipped in beneath the crack of the door, one that I kept to myself: *What do you mean I'm far from being a woman? I'm just like they are, I can do what they do, I can do it even better!*

Date: Tues. 20 Feb.
From: TaosUSA@gov.com
To: LincolnM@aol.com
I'm in Taos. I've always loved it here. I've asked your
dad to buy a home here and he refuses. I don't know
what in hell he's saving his money for. I have a theory:
you remember Flora, Fauna and Merriweather, the
three fairies who bestowed birth wishes on Sleeping
Beauty? I think some twisted fairy or spirit or some-
thing came to your father when he was born and sprin-
kled gray sand on him and said, "You will never see
anything but shades of gray, no color. And all foods will
taste the same, and things of beauty will escape you,
and you will hear a constant buzz like a loud fluores-
cent light that conceals the beauty of voices and water-
falls and birds, and everything will smell like unsalted
potatoes and you will live in the dark forever and ever."
What do you think, Lincoln? Is your dad alive? Or is
he dead? Please kick him when you see him and tell me
if he moves.
　　For the first time in my life I have too few hours in

my day. Everything I see and touch and taste and smell excites me. My life, once unsweetened oatmeal, is now salted anchovies. So unlike the past . . . back in the days when, if I didn't have some project in progress, some sort of creative outlet, I just floated from day to day, and I'd start to feel as cool and flat and tramped upon as the kitchen floor. I struggled to find something to be excited about: Remember my yoga period? And how you'd join me on the living-room floor each morning? Then I had my Tupperware-selling phase, then that diet where we reversed the day's meals, eating a heavy dinner for breakfast and a bowl of cereal for dinner. I hope, my sweet son, that you have found some front-burner, sanity-saving projects to keep your active mind alive. Anybody stuck at home has got to have some project or cause to keep them going when the kids and husband and life in general let them down. . . . . . . I'm hitting some galleries this afternoon to try and sell some of my paintings from my Carol-on-the-Lam series. My car is doing fine. She, too, is enjoying her new freedom. Love you. Mom.

Violet in bed, I opened my third Thai beer and wandered around the house, too buzzed to concentrate on a book. I pruned house plants and reorganized a corner in the living room that I was still unhappy with. It needed either a fuller plant or a larger book case.

Then, as often happens when I've had too much drink and not enough companionship, I got phone-happy and decided to call all my old friends in California, though, I soon discovered, the four-hour time difference meant most of them were either at happy hour or stuck in traffic.

Dad would be at work. I dialed the dealership.

"Lincoln?" he asked. "Is something wrong?"

"Just calling to talk. I usually call at home, but Mom's not there."

"No."

"Have you heard from her?"

"She's still e-mailing me."

"What does she say?"

"Doesn't she e-mail you?"

"No," I lied. "Not anymore. What does she say?"

"She's all over the goddamn place, in New Mexico right now. I've told everyone she's out visiting you and Josephine. . . . She hasn't talked with you?"

"No."

"Well if she does, tell her she can keep the damn car. God knows how many miles she's got on it now."

I pictured my dad beneath clinical fluorescent lights, sitting at his immaculate, walnut-Formica desk in his stark-white office decorated with nothing but an artificial shef-flera plant and plaques from groups such as the Rotary Club, Ford International, the Greater Bakersfield Chamber of Commerce. He always has eschewed anything that might reveal or catalog personal travels or family lineage or hobbies or desires. My father is very Puritan, seemingly afraid of physical details that might delight him even in the smallest way, as if pleasure will damn him straight to hell.

"Why do you think she ran away?" I asked.

"She didn't run away."

"Okay, then."

"Your mom's a romantic, Lincoln, she reads too many books, and she's got this crazy idea of a world out there that doesn't exist."

"Don't you think she might want someone to go get her? You think this might be a test of some kind?"

"I think your mother likes to travel, and she knows I don't like to take time off to travel. Maybe this'll get it out of her system."

"Jesus, Dad, you sound so cold about it all."

He covered the phone to say something to someone who had walked into his office, his voice sounding as if he were talking into a pillow.

"I'm not going to be the asshole here, Lincoln. Your mother is an unusual woman. It's not easy to live with her. Between you and me, sometimes I feel more like her father than her husband. I take care of her, Lincoln. I try my very best to provide for her and keep her happy, but your mother's got a huge goddamned appetite. She tires me out."

I lay down on the floor in the middle of the family room, looking up at the ceiling twenty-two feet away. How would I change those bulbs when they burned out?

Christmas bulbs.

Tulips.

Kissing.

Bedsheets need washing.

How do hotels get their sheets so tight?

"You do love her—don't you?" I asked.

"Of course I love her."

"Do you ever show her?"

"Of course I do."

Drunk and fueled by caregiver solidarity, I'd started pushing my father into a corner, much further than ever before. I thought of how I gave up my incredible entrée last weekend at Mephisto's because Jo didn't like the trout she ordered. I thought of how I send photos of Violet to Jo's parents every month so they can chart her growth. I thought of how I missed my HBO special on Indonesian cooking so I could take dinner and Violet down to the hospital to see her mother for a whopping fifteen minutes of bonding. There's a reason women read more than men. They get stuck in undesirable locales and situations more often—soccer fields, hospital rooms, bedsides—and a book helps pass the time.

"I don't mean that little bullshit kiss in the kitchen every morning," I said. "Do you tell Mom how much you appreciate her? All those meals and ironed shirts and curiosity about your day at the office? Do you have any idea of the sacrifices she's made, any idea what she gives up every day to keep your life running so smoothly?"

"You've been drinking," he said. "I can tell."

"I've been drinking," I replied. "I can tell."

"Power's off," I said, seconds after stepping into the house from the garage. On a rare family outing, Jo included in this, we'd driven over to Niagara Falls for the day.

"How can you tell?" Jo asked.

"I just know it."

I noted the absence of the refrigerator's hum, the general dead stillness of a house with no electricity buzzing through its nervous system of wires. I'd been in this house full-time for eight months, and I was omniscient caretaker, intimately familiar with this four-thousand-square-foot creature we lived in, its rhythms and odors and sounds. Earlier this year, I knew the heater was going to konk out a week before it happened. I could just feel it, or rather hear it, a barely perceptible "ting" on each revolution of the blower cylinder. Jo said I imagined it. She heard nothing. I heard stress and friction in what should have been a fluid, circular pattern.

Walking into the hallway, I heard the voices: Patty. A man. A second woman. I walked into the kitchen and saw the three of them in swimming suits on the snowy deck, bent over the control panel of the hot tub, blindly, thoughtlessly pushing at the controls like chimps in a laboratory.

I whipped open the French door, and the three of them shot up to full posture and turned toward me.

"Sweet holy shit mother of Jesus," Patty said. "You scared the hell out of me."

"What the hell are you doing here?" I asked.

"I thought you were gonna be gone."

I noted their tally for fun, lining the edge of the hot tub: Nine amber bottles of Schlitz beer, most of them empty.

"What the hell tripped the breaker . . . and who the hell are you?"

"This is Nancy and Bobby." Patty picked up a towel and wrapped it around her middle section like a skirt. Jo and Violet, knowing me very well, stood back and watched the scene in silence. "Me and Nancy have been friends since high school."

"Bobby the convict?"

"He got out of jail yesterday. We're celebrating."

"And probably robbing me blind."

"Hey! My boyfriend's no crook."

"Oh, I'm sorry, I forget. He was doing some consulting work in prison."

"He wasn't in prison. He was in jail."

"Whatever."

As did the woman, Bobby stood silently, obviously accustomed to his girlfriend defending him. He was built like Patty, a no-neck, stocky frame I associate with wooden African fetishes. He was attempting to grow a mustache though didn't have the follicle density to do it right, making it look as if he'd been playing grown-up with his mother's mascara.

"You didn't even ask me, Patty."

"You woulda said no."

"Yes, I would have, and do you know why? Because there's a liability issue here. Bobby here falls and breaks his back and you sue me. I know your type, Patty, that's exactly what you'd do."

"You're crazy." She turned to her friend. "I told you he was frickin' crazy."

"But you know what pisses me off more?" I said. "That you sneaked. Just like you sneak with the pepperoni and sneak with the coin jar and lie about Violet's exercise regimen."

Patty, who'd seen Jo only twice before, walked past her, toward the stairs. "I don't know how you live with him," she said. "He's a mean son of a bitch."

They disappeared around the side of the house, and I stood on the deck, surveying the damage, which reminded me of the orgiastic scene in the *Musicians of Breman*, which I'd read to Violet the week before, a story in which a no-good jackass and his animal friends take over a family's house and proceed to suck it dry of all food and drink, tossing peelings and bones over their shoulders during their journey of gluttony. Indeed, a plate of chicken bones sat on the wooden decking, next to an emptied bag of Frito's (brought in by Patty) and an opened jar of olive pâté, which they'd tasted and tossed aside.

"Do you think she's coming back?" Jo asked.

"What do you mean?"

"Do you think she'd already quit in her mind, and this was her last hurrah and chance to get you back?"

"I'm not that lucky."

"If you hate her that much, Lincoln—and it's obvious you do—then why don't you fire her?"

"I'm not good at confrontations."

"Ha!"

"I'm not good at civil confrontations. Why don't you do it?"

"Because she's your direct report."

"Thanks a lot, Jo," I said, starting to pick up the beer bottles. "But I want that horticulturalist job with the village, and I can't do it without her. She's got me by the short hairs."

Nan and Joanne were waiting for me at the corner. "Sorry I'm late," I said. "I overslept."

"Bad night?" Nan asked.

"Huge fight," I answered, pulling my gloves from my pockets.

"So tell us about it," Joanne said.

"I don't want to talk about it. Most of the time it's my fault anyway."

"We'll be the judge of that," Nan said.

"Was it child-related or just general insensitivity?" Joanne asked.

As we puffed our way in the dark down Saddle Creek Run, I recalled for them the night before, when Jo came home early and found Violet crying in her room. I had told Violet she couldn't come downstairs until she picked up her toys. Jo told me she was too young to clean her room, and she helped her finish the task. I told her she was unraveling all the wild strings of behavior that I spend my entire day trying to braid and tie and tame. "You want a spoiled child that no one wants to play with? Then keep this up," I said.

"You're overreacting, Linc," Jo said.

"No. You don't know what a day is like in this house without some standards of good behavior. There has to be one boss here, and it's me. There's a reason everyone says she's so polite; it didn't happen by accident."

"So Violet's got one parent, is that it?"

"No. But you've got to support what I do. I have to live with her all day. If we don't enforce the rules every damn second then she starts to test me. And test me and test me and test me. And then my day is absolute hell. And then you wonder why I'm in such a bad mood when you get home!"

Jo stormed into the bedroom and slammed the door. She didn't talk to me when I came to bed an hour later. She pretended to be asleep, but I knew she wasn't because she snores when she's asleep. Her allergies had gotten worse in Rochester; it was all the dampness and mold. I'd tried to get her to start taking shots. I even went as far as to make an appointment with the allergist, which she missed. When I asked her about it, she told me to quit trying to run her life, that the harder I tried to control her, the madder and more distant she became. You don't understand, I said. I'm just trying to help. Compassionate caregivers always come off as control freaks.

As I relayed the story, both women continually shook their heads, as if I were describing a movie they'd already seen.

"You're right," Joanne said. "You screwed up."

"She's wrong, and you're wrong," Nan said.

"She needs to be more sensitive to the autonomy of the primary caregiver," Joanne said.

"And you need to quit being such an asshole," added Nan.

"I know, I know, I know, I know," I said.

"I used to be a working mom, Linc," Nan said, "and I felt as small as mouse turds when the nanny would correct me on something. You've got to tread carefully in these waters."

"So what do I do?" I asked.

"Stop rubbing her nose in it," Joanne said. "Don't make her feel so ignorant about child-rearing, let her feel like she's contributing."

"Even when you think she's doing it in a wrong way," Joanne added. "You've got to choose your battles carefully."

"So what you're saying is I need to pretend that she's doing the right thing and that I agree—even if it's not true."

They both nodded their heads.

"And then you quietly step in and fix the situation after they leave."

"But that's lying," I said.

"It's not lying," Nan said. "It's called keeping the peace and protecting self-esteem, and that's your job as the caregiver. . . . And that reminds me of something I wanted to tell you last time—and then that will be the end of today's lecture."

"What?"

"You intimated that it was unfair for Jo to want the family room picked up when she gets home."

"So?" I said. "You don't think that's archaic in these modern times? Housewives don't serve their men like that anymore."

"If you worked outside the home all day it would be a different matter. But you're home, Linc, and you can control these things, and there's nothing wrong with reducing the chaos in your wife's life. And if she wants a clean family room, then that's okay."

"Did you see that article in the newspaper yesterday?" Joanne asked. "The one about executives with a spouse at home?"

"I did," Nan said. "What was it again? I can't remember."

"It said that executives with a spouse at home earn something like twenty percent more."

"Yeah?" I said.

"And I know it's because they have less chaos at home. That's got to be the reason."

It was true that, without even trying, I'd grown to take pride in taking such good care of Jo. My self-imposed personal challenge, created by guilt and boredom, was to anticipate her every need, and I would get down on myself if I noticed that she had had to break down and purchase new panty hose or a tooth brush. I'd been at home long enough now that I could troll the aisles of the grocery store, pass the personal hygiene section and know instinctively—Was it by osmosis? Some internal clock?—that she soon would be running out of Soft n' Dri, and that I needed to pluck another from the shelf and set it in her medicine cabinet, ready and waiting for her when the need arose some time that week. My mother most likely would say playing such a subservient, eager-to-please role was humiliating and denigrating. I guess I would tell her it is denigrating only if you feel denigrated by doing it, and I do not. Lately Jo has been most thankful and forthcoming with her praise, and that has made all the difference in the world.

We turned from River Ranch Drive onto Fox Trot Run, the street with the house where the guy works out with weights in the garden-level basement. I've noticed that we always slow down at this spot. From here, we would hit the bike path by the creek and follow it up the park, then disperse from there. These walks were never long enough. In my months at home, in this female world, I had learned that I could talk with women for hours. They discuss things that matter, almost always tethering their conversations to humanity. They listen better, scrutinize more with their eyes, they notice not only what is said but also *how* it is said: Yes can mean no, no can mean maybe, perhaps can mean tomorrow or next year or never, depending on what the eyes were saying, where the hands were held, the time of day it was uttered. Women share more because they're not afraid to be vulnerable or to sway or bend or change. Testosterone makes men hard; we are rigid so as to deflect any foreign, potentially frightening thought that might bump into us.

"So who's making what for dinner tonight?" I asked, breaking the silence.

A few weeks back we'd started a mental cooking exercise. Pretending she was snowbound and unable to go to
the store, each walker would divulge what she had in the
vegetable crisper, freezer and pantry, and the group would
brainstorm possible meals. No one was better at this than I.

"Okay, let me go first because my case is the most
hopeless," Nan said. "Cleaned my refrigerator out last
night. I'm going to the store this morning. I've got two oranges. Period."

"That's impossible!" Joanne said.

"Got any olives—black olives?" I asked.

"A jar of Greek olives, maybe."

"Perfect. . . . Any shallots?"

"A regular onion."

"Good enough."

"What's in your meat drawer?" Joanne asked.

"Bacon."

"What kind of cheese?" I asked.

"Colby. And a little feta."

"Nothing frozen at all?" I asked.

"Some leftover chicken legs."

"Got it," I said, and both women looked at me, awaiting
my answer. "Dice the onion, oranges, mince the olives and
some garlic and mix them all together, maybe a little extra-
virgin, salt and pepper."

"What about the cheese?"

"Save it for last, crumble the feta on top and serve it
with a chicken leg beside."

We had reached the bike path, and I remembered that I had rising bread dough that needed to be punched down.

"Do you guys mind if I run this last quarter-mile?" I said.

"You joining us on Thursday?" Nan asked.

"Absolutely."

My face red and hot, I climbed the stairs of the back deck, on my way to the kitchen door, and noticed paint peeling on the gable near the fireplace.

Walk the roof and survey condition of shingles.

Clean out gutters.

Leaky roofs.

Five solid weeks of no bed-wetting!

Turn mattress in master.

Princess and the Pea.

Resubscribe to horticulture magazines.

Jo was sitting at the table in her white terry-cloth bathrobe, reading the newspaper and drinking a cup of coffee that I had brewed before leaving. She looked up at me and smiled.

"Nice walk?" she asked.

"Did you know I've lost nine pounds?" I said, smiling because I had told her the same thing every morning for three days now.

"I think I knew that, yes. . . . You didn't listen to the messages last night, did you?"

"I don't think so, why?"

"There's one that might interest you."

"What is it?"

"Just go listen. There's only one."

I walked over and poked the replay button. Though the man's voice sounded monotone and unemotional as the computer-generated voice on National Weather Service storm alerts, the content of the message gave it the lightness of the hallelujah chorus. Starting one week from Wednesday, I would be the new chief horticulturalist for the Village of Pittsford.

"Yo!" I cried. "Yo, yo, yo, yo, yo! I got it! I goddamn got it, got it, got it!"

Jo walked up and wrapped her arms around my waist.

"Man, do I ever need this!" I said. "You have no idea how perfect, perfect, perfect, perfect this job is for me."

I felt Jo pulling herself into me. "Perfect for *us*," she whispered into my ear. "You're repeating words just like your daughter."

"I want to go tell Violet," I said.

"You're adorable."

"Jo . . ."

"And Violet's asleep."

"Yeah."

"And we've got twenty minutes."

"Yeah?"

"Yeah," she said, pulling me toward the stairs.

"Don't you want me to shower?"

"I don't mind *fresh* sweat," she said.

Time and again, over the past ten months, fresh spring rolls have been my salvation. They're a snap to throw together, and everyone thinks you've gone to such extremes because you're feeding them something they can get only in a Vietnamese restaurant. I am making spring rolls again tonight, the third time this month.

Violet and I had spent the afternoon building a fort in the living room, a tent town comprised of six tables, another half dozen chairs and a collection of blankets and sheets held together by duct tape and clothes pins. Time escaped us, and I suddenly realized that three hours had passed—six-thirty!—and Jo had said she'd be home early for dinner because of a late-night meeting with the building-maintenance staff.

"Come on, sweetheart," I said. "I need your help making dinner."

The only cooked meat I had was leftover sea bass from two nights earlier. I handed Violet a butter knife and the fish. "I need this in little pieces . . . not teeny-tiny but about the size of Barbie's purse."

"Oh, Daddy, you want me to use a knife?"

"This is a safe knife, Violet. This is the only knife you must ever use until you're a grown-up."

I boiled the cellophane noodles and blanched the rice papers, then set up a manufacturing assembly line.

"Did you know this is how they make toys?" I asked. "People stand in a line, and each person adds something to the toy until it's all done."

Since the plate-sized rice papers were sticky and hard to handle, I laid them out flat. Violet then added fish, fresh basil, cilantro, bean sprouts and a forkful of cellophane noodles before I rolled them up.

We were halfway finished when the phone rang. Violet answered, and a quizzical look appeared on her face.

"It's no one, Daddy."

I took the phone from her and pushed star-six-nine: *555-4528.*

I dialed Marilyn's number back and let it ring ten times but got no answer.

"Come on, sweetie, we're going over to Marilyn's."

"Why?"

"I just feel like something's wrong."

Violet and I ran across the two yards separating the homes. The garage door was open. At the door to the inside, I could hear Steven shouting—"You goddamn bitch, let me in!"—and an occasional thud, and the sound of splintering wood.

"Violet, run back home and lock the door, okay?"

"Daddy, this is scary."

"Just go home, and when your mommy gets back tell

her where I am. Now run. Go!" I said, swatting her on the fanny.

I opened the door, walked through the kitchen, following the sounds of what I soon would discover was a seven- or nine-iron penetrating then being pulled from the bathroom door.

Startled, Steven looked up at me from the end of the dark hall.

"Who the fuck are you? Get the fuck out of here!"

"Linc?" Marilyn yelled from the other side of the door.

He turned toward me, raising the club. "So you're the asshole who's been dickin' my wife!"

His face and neck were inflamed and looked like poached salmon. He was so shit-faced he hadn't even taken off his golf shoes, and the steel cleats had scrawled lines into the maple floor.

"Take it easy, man," I said. "Put the club down. I don't want a scene."

"Get the fuck outta here. Go fuck somebody else's wife."

"You don't need to talk like that. You're saying some pretty nasty things that aren't true."

"Go fuck yourself! Get the fuck outta here!"

"I can't do that. Not until you calm down."

He raised his club and took a step toward me.

"I wouldn't do that, buddy. I'm a helluva lot bigger than you are."

Yet onward he charged, club in the air. Thanks to his extreme drunkenness, his advance was as anemic as a staged fight in a high-school play. The club came down, and I simply grabbed it with one hand and punched him in the gut with the other. He doubled over, unceremoniously fell to his hands and knees and started vomiting on the floor.

"Marilyn!" I snapped. "Marilyn, get out here!"

She emerged from the bathroom, her face red and wet from tears. She walked up to her husband and looked at him on the floor, tentative but curious, as if he were fresh kill in a hunt and might make one last deadly swipe with a paw.

"Get your kids. Where are they—upstairs?"

She nodded.

"Take them to your parents."

"No," she said. "I don't need to do that."

"Don't be so stupid," I said.

Steven lay on his side like a fetus, his head situated in a way that the pool of vomit looked like a brownish-pink word balloon coming out of his mouth.

"He's passed out."

"And then he'll come to and beat the shit out of you. Has this happened before?"

"Not like this."

"Go to your mom's."

"No, really. It's over now, I can tell."

"What the hell is wrong with you?"

"It's going to be all right, I know it."

"Jesus Christ, Marilyn, will you for once take charge of your life," I said. "All you do is bitch about this guy and allude to how miserable he makes you, and you never do anything to change it."

"I can't!"

"The hell you can't. If he's that bad then leave the son of a bitch. Go cater again. But quit whining and do something to make yourself happy. And start thinking about your kids a little bit more, would you? You think they like watching this shit?"

"You don't understand," she said.

"No, I sure as hell do not," I said. "I don't understand you. I don't understand my mother. I don't understand why you can't just grab the bull by the horns and take charge of your own goddamn life."

As I spoke this, however, I knew it was more difficult than that. It is easier, even expected, for a man to seek and hunt down what he wants. (I wanted a job, I found a job.) Yet, unfair as it may be, a woman who aggressively chases what she wants is seen as a self-serving bitch, a threat to the family, as my mother might now be perceived by my father's friends. She did, however, wait until I was grown and gone.

Marilyn looked down at her husband then brought her hand to her cheek as if comforting a fresh slap. I moved to comfort with a hug, but she shook her head no. I was the wrong gender for this moment. I had just defended her from one of my own.

"Please go," she said without looking up.

I walked home knowing we most likely never would cook together again, yet I wasn't saddened or much surprised because, over the past month or so, I had felt the curtain closing on this relationship. I'd grown tired of being unhappy and Marilyn had not, and if I stuck around she would drag me back down with her. Depression is a funny thing. You really don't know you're treading water in pitch darkness until someone has yanked you out and pulled you up onto the deck of the boat, and all of a sudden you're aware of the warm sunlight on your skin and the smell and taste of salt, sensations that simultaneously seem foreign yet oddly familiar.

Meal-in-One Spring Rolls

1 package rice papers, used for spring roll
   wrappers (Can be bought in most Asian markets.
   These have a long shelf life and can be kept on
   hand for several months.)
1 cup fresh cilantro, chopped
1 cup fresh basil, chopped
2 cups leftover cooked meat from the refrigerator
   (can be fish, beef, pork, chicken or a
   combination)
2 cups cellophane noodles or angel-hair pasta,
   cooked, cooled and drained
   Sweetened chili sauce and hot chili sauce (Both
   can be bought in Asian groceries and kept in the
   refrigerator for many months.)

It is easy to feel intimidated when cooking rice papers the first time. Don't be. It's not that difficult. Remember that everyone rips some of the soggy, cooked papers.

Simply drop a rice paper into an inch of softly boiling water in a skillet, gently poking it beneath the water with a spatula or wooden spoon. Cook for 30 seconds, then scoop out and drop into a waiting bowl of cool water. This stops the cooking process and keeps them from sticking together. Make as many as you need, and be sure to make extras because some will break during rolling.

Lay each cooked rice paper on the counter and put a collection of the remaining ingredients (excluding the sauces) in the center. Fold two ends toward the middle, then bring up the bottom flap and lay it over the mixture. Start rolling. Experiment. Everyone tends to develop their own rolling technique.

Dip into sauces served at tableside.

Date: Thur. 9 March

From: Mountpacknmail@Telly.dpt.com

To: LincolnM@aol.com

There's no public access computer at the library in Butte, Montana; I'm at one of those Kinko's-like places that makes copies and sends packages. Fascinating place, Butte. I came here because of something I saw in the Times. It's a ghost town of sorts, used to be one of the world's largest copper-mining operations, poisoned pools of water sitting everywhere, empty mine shafts, about 30,000 people now and it used to be closer to 100K. (Your father taught me what "K" meant.) Met the most fascinating man in the visitors' bureau; name is Ben Arter (the man I read about in the Times) and he's trying to convince Congress to turn the entire city into a national park for historical reasons—you know, preserve a piece of America's industrial history. I had dinner with him last night, sketched his cat as a gift.

This city stirs me. People here feel used and abandoned but their pride and roots are intact because their families have lived here for generations, and they remain here even though the world has sucked them dry and moved on. I can't decide if this is brave or pathetic.

I'm having a heyday painting buildings here, abandoned and limestone, their windows punched out so they look like dark tired eyes. I used to feel this way, Lincoln, like these buildings. A lot of women from my generation do. You get married, you immediately have children (or child, as in my case). Your family runs you wild, sucking your time, passion, energy, everything. In almost every culture on the planet, Mom is the building that harbors the family, and people just don't value architecture like they should. You wear it out, you move into another. Kind of like a car, I guess.

I guess by now you know that my car isn't the issue here. I know we trade them every two years because once it hits 10,000 the blue-book resale value drops dramatically. Your father's told me that ad nauseum. He's a car dealer, what else should I expect? Trade your car in like a good girl, Carol, right? I don't think so, not this time. This car—especially now—is my cloud, it's a covered wagon. Did you know it's so big I can fully stretch out and lay down in the back seat? I'm going to drive my blue Lincoln until the sun bleaches it from blue, to gray, to silver, to white, to invisible, and then I will drive it up to heaven like a chariot, and st. peter will say, Oh, Carol, I see you've brought your car, and what a lovely, roomy car it is.

I wonder if your father is clipping his own toenails, or

*if he's waiting for me to come back and do it for him like
I always do. I'm not mad at your father, Lincoln; I pity
him. He's the product of an era. I hope to god, for future
generations of women, that the concrete-face, emotionally dead Fifties man will be a blip in history. Like the
Edsel. Love you.*

Though I had a desk in the village hall planning department, I did most of my paperwork and phoning in my office at home. The village administrator, a woman, was
understanding of my needs for flexibility, and she had no
problem where I did my job as long as I got it done. This
suited me well because I did not want to start wearing a
shirt and tie. I could breeze in, the eccentric artist from
California, wearing Teva sandals and wool socks, and they
would politely smile, hand me my messages and paperwork and send me on my way.

I had learned that the Stuart Cable, a vine-variety lilac
known for its pale, creamy violet hue, had been grafted
right here in Pittsford some hundred years ago. I'd convinced my boss that Pittsford needed a signature flower,
and that the Stuart Cable was the most appropriate, subtle
in color yet with bounteous blossoms, an overall vintage
appearance, like something from a sepia-toned photograph. I'd also talked him into new signs marking the village limits. Surrounded by Stuart Cables, of course, these

would be simple, steel plaques, like those on an eighteenth-century cemetery entrance. They would say, simply, "Pittsford, Established 1796."

I had spent the better part of the entire morning on the phone, talking with suppliers, and I was speaking with a man in Belgium when I heard the garage door open, that vibrating hum and the clickety clack of steel wheels passing joints, an altogether foreign sound at that time of day.

I heard Jo's key in the lock, then her heels on the slate floor, then nothing. She'd ascended the carpeted stairs to . . . the bathroom? No, I could tell from the creaks in the floor that she was in Violet's room. I heard her open then shut a drawer. What on earth could she be doing? And home! At this time of day! I hoped she would remember to turn off the light.

On her way out, she poked her head into my office.

"Yes," I said to the supplier, waving her in. "I would need at least three hundred. Yes, three hundred."

As he answered, I mouthed a message to Jo. "What's wrong?"

She dangled a pair of pink Little Mermaid panties in the air. "Violet peed her pants," she whispered, smiling, then blew me a kiss and left.

Ten minutes later I hung up, quickly retrieved voice-mail messages and discovered that Jo had called me four times in the past hour, trying to reach me for this emergency. I dialed her cell phone number to apologize.

"Lincoln, I don't mind at all," she said. "I like being needed. It makes me feel good."

"Yeah, but I feel horrible," I said. "My little girl peed her pants in front of her peers, and she needed me, and I wasn't there."

"But I was, so it doesn't matter."

Still, I felt guilty. The headmistress had had to bother Jo, who did not have time in her day to spend ninety minutes picking up and delivering clean underwear. Then again, neither did I.

Though I loved my job, it already was pulling and stretching me, and I'd started looking for shortcuts. I stopped hanging the laundry outside; everything got thrown into the dryer, even the nylons and Violet's pink silky nighties. Dust bunnies roamed freely across the smooth maple prairies of our home. My kitchen knives needed sharpening. I'd started putting my wooden spoons in the dishwasher instead of washing them by hand. This would cause them to dry and splinter, I knew, but these were choices I'd had to make.

Ellington Elementary School is a grand Georgian Revival building that last year, thanks to its students' Messianic mothers, was included on the National Register of Historic Places. Seemingly every inch of its wooden white trim is perfectly maintained. The golden, cherry-wood doors are so polished and clean they seem to glow like portals to a warmer world. The only problem with Ellington Elementary is the landscaping. That sprawling building, stretching for half a block, has but one yew bush on its entire front side. One. It looks as naked as a man's shaved leg. I do not understand it.

Ellington sits right on historic Main Street, and when people drive in from the city to shop at our overpriced women's boutiques and gourmet food stores they pass right by the school. It gives an impression that we don't care about appearance.

I asked and asked and asked and finally gained approval to approach the principal about letting the village landscape the grounds for him.

"Why would I want to do that?" he asked me over the phone.

"Because it looks like hell," I said.

Finally, after four weeks, he agreed to meet with me on a Saturday morning at McGruder's, a diner on Main Street. Jo was downtown working until four or so. Patty was due at 11:30, with my meeting scheduled to begin promptly at 11:45.

At 11:40 I called her. "Where the hell are you?"

"I'm sick. Throwin' up."

In the background I could hear Bob Barker on *The Price Is Right*.

"This won't do, Patty. You've got to get here. Now!"

"My brother can't bring me."

"I'll come get you."

"You want your daughter to get this stuff? What kind of dad are you?"

"This is unacceptable, Patty."

"So's throwin' up."

I slammed the receiver into its cradle, creating enough of a reverberation that a book from atop the refrigerator fell to the floor, open to a recipe for a saffron lobster hash. I envisioned holding a lobster over the steam, watching it writhe back and forth in a desperate little dance. I decided that the lobster was Patty. "Dance all you want to," I said in my fantasy. "This is what you get." And I dropped her into the bubbling water, which swallowed all but the tip of one antennae that seemed to point up at me like an accusing finger.

I couldn't take Violet with me, that was too unprofessional even for a Saturday. I was furious, but what could I do? I called and left a message for the principal at the diner then walked upstairs to my office with intentions of finally attacking the blueprint for the labyrinth hedge I'd talked the village board into letting me plant at Hazel-Abel park.

I passed Violet's room on the way and peeked inside. She had set up runways for models and was strutting her Barbies up and down a shiny row of Dr. Seuss books. The Veterinarian Barbie I had bought her was wearing a lime-green evening gown fringed along the neck with pink marabou. I'd been so busy I had had little play time with Violet, and I missed the unstructured hours in which I would learn her peeves and tastes and passions. What was she pretending? What was she thinking?

"Hello, sweetheart," I said.

"Daddy!"

"Why don't you get dressed up?"

"You mean fancy?"

"Fancy like Barbie," I said.

"Why?"

"It's a surprise."

I decided to make the most out of my jacket and tie. We'd go have tea at the downtown Hyatt and work on the table manners I'd been meaning to pay more attention to— napkins in the lap, scones held with one hand, not two.

Violet emerged from her room wearing a short-sleeve pink dress inappropriate for the still-cool weather and the hat my mom had made her, wide-rimmed white straw with baseball-sized poppies glued to the band. On her feet were purple socks stuffed into clear plastic Cinderella slippers from the dress-up box.

"How do I look, Daddy?" she asked.

"Oh, honey," I said, my eyes absorbing her. Her pink goose bump–covered arms, and her mother's blond hair that falls down her back, and that smile with lips the color of melted raspberry ice cream, and those Chinese-like feet that keep us hiking for hours through mall after mall as we search for elusive narrow sizes.

"You take my breath away, honey." And on the way out the door, I plucked her polar fleece coat from the foyer closet.

The first block party in the new neighborhood's four-year history had been organized by a pair of overly social empty nesters who own and run a real-estate company. They have names that rhyme, something like Mary and Barry or Sue and Lou. I did not know most of the men, and neither did Jo, but this didn't seem to bother her. She soon melted in with a group of four, two of them doctors who, after discovering who she was, began drilling her on problems with the radiology department at the hospital.

I carried my rotini with bacon and ancho-chili cream sauce over to the food table, where I lingered, checking out what others had brought. From here, I saw Steven and Marilyn approaching in the distance, she carrying a white casserole dish the two of us had filled time and again with our creations. We had not spoken since the night of the clubbing.

Oddly enough, it was Steven who approached me before his wife.

"Hello, Linc," he said, shooting me a smile that, in this context, seemed macabre.

Rod Serling in Twilight Zone.

The pedestrian crossing near the school and the problems with speeders.

Did he remember? Surely he remembered.

The versatility of a golf club.

Cave man.

Carlsbad Caverns in New Mexico.

Had I put too many ancho chilis in the sauce?

"I'm sure you cooked up something good today."

I nodded. "Your kids helped me," I said.

When the weather is fine, as it is today, I shell peas on

the front porch, sitting in the cool spring sunlight, eating the ones Violet and I drop on the concrete. Usually we have company when we do this, the kids of the neighborhood lured by the sweetness of the raw peas and the glee of opening something and finding a line of cuddly, green little orbs reminiscent of newborn baby toes. I've learned that kids love to see food in its raw state, the silk tassels of sweet corn, the bumpy shells of peanuts. Because Marilyn and I had not spoken since that night, I was relieved when Dax and Sarah saw Violet and me and the peas and ran over to join us. Next came ten-year-old Kate and another nine-ish boy I didn't recognize, maybe someone's grandson. Ever since I started my walks with Joanne and Nan, it seemed as if an embargo had been lifted on the household of the male interloper, and kids were free to come and go as they pleased. In upscale neighborhoods such as mine, most parents don't let their children do chores, and my lure was that I would let these kids wash my truck, help me make pasta, mow the grass, sweep out the garage, as if these were novel activities they'd never known.

Marilyn walked up to the table.

"What did you make?" I asked her, feeling awkward, as if this were a first encounter after sleeping together for the first time.

"Tamales and green chili," she said.

"Pork?"

"Of course."

A male voice summoned Steven, who reluctantly left

the two of us alone. We spoke with no eye contact, using the table full of food as an all-consuming visual distraction.

"So how have you been?" I asked.

"Fine. And you?"

"Really busy, not much time for fun."

"I know what you mean."

"Busy?"

"I'm redoing Sarah's room," she said. "And then the family room."

Ah, I thought, redecorating, the time-filler and passion-anesthetic for stay-at-home mothers who have the support of weekly housecleaners. In my ten months at home, I'd continually been surprised at how often entire rooms would get make-overs, even in homes just two or three years old, projects financed by husbands feeling guilty for abandoning their family for golf outings and fishing trips, or for trying to maim or kill their wives with a nine-iron. Over the year I'd watched a woman six doors down, named Carolyn Something, who nearly every weekday would carry outside and set into her Mercedes trunk a throw pillow or cliché landscape oil in gilt frame, then speed away and spend her day driving around town, searching out swatches and paint chips and lamps that just might tie everything in her life together, but in the end she's dissatisfied again, and returns everything the next morning, only to search again. In these households there always seems to be something missing, something these women seek in antiques stores and fabric shops and furniture galleries that might, if added to the right room in the right way, bring harmony, elusive perfection, a missing ingredient.

"Wallpaper?" I asked.

"In Sarah's room, yes."

"What kind?"

"She wanted pink ballerinas, but I found a lovely floral."

Steven interrupted us. "Marilyn, I want you to meet somebody." And, then, turning to me. "See you around."

I looked around for another human connection. I really had no one to latch onto. Nan had gone to Idaho for her great-grandmother's birthday party. Joanne was speaking with the icy snow-mountain woman. On the far side of the driveway was a group of men whose conversation had drifted from finances to basketball to the rumors of more reorganizing at Kodak. I wanted to join the conversation but had been out of the male loop for so long that I felt self-conscious, like the new boy in the classroom who is afraid to step into an existing group of friends because he fears rejection and doesn't yet know the cultural rules and expectations and interests. But when I heard the conversation turn toward leaf blowers, I saw an entrée.

"I have a McElroy MaxFlo," I said.

"Hardcore!" remarked one guy.

"I can balance a basketball with it," I said.

"I bet you can."

"No. Really. Wanna see?"

"This I gotta see."

I ran down to the house, strapped it onto my back and walked back to the picnic, bouncing the basketball. Not wanting to disturb the larger group, I motioned for the men to join me on a driveway two homes away.

"Okay," I said, throwing the ball to one of the guys. "Up in the air. Right here."

He tossed it up, I revved to the max and the ball stopped on its way back down, balanced on an invisible arm of air.

The men were impressed, and soon a larger crowd gathered, almost all of them men. I let each of them have a turn, and in the end ran the blower for so long that it ran out of gas.

"My wife won't let me have one with a piston motor," said one man named Gary. "She's worried about my ears."

"Duh," said another. "So what about ear plugs?"

And another guy: "They always have to complain about something. They wouldn't be women if they didn't bitch—right?"

From this point on, the conversation most likely would take a direction I did not want to follow. I had no desire to bitch-bash, and I quietly ducked out of the circle, though I should have stayed and enlightened these guys. I should have explained that one reason their women assert control over seemingly tiny things is because they feel as if their husbands have broad-sweeping, godlike control over their lives. I should have told them that the world would be a less civil, less beautiful place if it weren't for their stay-at-home wives, that we would forget to use napkins and pardon ourselves for belching. We'd sleep in sour, dirty sheets and our senses would start to shut down because they'd be unhappy with their surroundings. Litter would accumulate in gutters, school standards would plummet, playground equipment would go unfixed and pose dangers. Fewer of us would get presents or fresh fruit or whimsical surprises from Target. I wanted to tell them that the reason they get hounded by their women is because they truly care about the world we live in, that they're the dispensers of the details that keep us human. And if some woman didn't like the idea of a shirtless neighbor mowing his yard it's because in her mind she already sees the world teetering on the edge of civility, and bare chests and spitting on sidewalks and gaudy architecture and unmowed weeds just might push us one notch further toward another Dark Age.

"Linc!"

It was Joanne, waving me over toward a cluster of women. I started to walk over, and as I approached they suddenly grew quiet, like a group of girls on the playground.

"I was telling them about *passiflora*. Can you show them?"

"Now?"

"If you don't mind."

My mutant, aggressive specimen had grown to nearly fifty feet long, yet its journey appeared to be winding down. Over the past several months, the plant had inched from dining room into kitchen into foyer into hallway, then back into dining room. For the first time in almost a year it had left its lofty position near the ceiling and begun descending the wall, curiously making a beeline for the terracotta pot, the mother ship that fed its growth. Home. Was she finished exploring or would she take off again? And why had I allowed her such freedom and voraciousness? She seemed to be looking for something, I wanted to help her find it, so I let her explore as only a plant can do, leaving a long, fresh appendage in her wake, forever tied to and reliant upon her past travels but always moving onward, toward something new.

With a few hours' warning, corporate had summoned Jo to Nashville for an overnight meeting. She called from her office and left a somewhat pleading voice mail, asking if I could possibly throw together a suitcase with all the necessities, including a white silk blouse that I would have to pick up at the dry cleaners.

Mission accomplished, I took Violet grocery shopping. We were walking into the house, fourteen pregnant plastic bags suspended from my arms, when the phone began to ring. It was Jo, calling from the airport to thank me for pulling through, especially for clearing that extra hurdle of the silk blouse. Except there was a problem: I had forgotten to pick up the goddamn blouse. Jo had bra, clean panties, makeup, even tampons because I knew there was a

chance she'd start her period in the next twenty-four
hours, but she had no clean shirt, and she never can wear
the same shirt two days in a row because she is genetically
predisposed to dripping something from lunch down her
front.

Guilt! Would it never leave me alone? Twice now I had
let my family down, and it was not because I'd refused to
alter my standards. Indeed I had, more than I ever thought
possible. At Jo's urging, I had started using paper towels
instead of cloth napkins. Breakfast cereal bowls often
would now linger in the sink until after dinner. Violet was
watching more TV. I started to ignore squeaky hinges and
dried grape jelly on the drawer pulls. The bills had been ac-
cumulating in my basket like early-October leaves. Usually
I paid them every Sunday night after Violet had gone
to bed.

Once my family's strong, predictable safety net, I now
felt like the trapeze artist himself, flying from bar to bar,
grasping at any line that might swing my way in hopes of
staying afloat.

Something was up with Patty, I could tell. Ever since the hot-tub incident, she'd been too nice to me and too nice to Violet. She'd grown unnaturally sweet, as cloying as saccharine on the bare tongue: *Oh, yes, yes, my little snuggle bug, do you want to make some pudding with Patty? I just love you, love you to pieces!* I knew it was for show because after saying something like this she'd look up to make sure I was watching. I can't believe she doesn't know that I know how stupid she is.

She'd also stopped looking at me in the eye. I increasingly mistrusted her, so I decided to spy. I hid my voice-activated tape recorder in the clay chicken on top of the refrigerator, and I left for the day to work from my desk at village hall.

That afternoon, after Patty's brother came to pick her up in his big blue pickup, I sat down at the kitchen table to listen. As suspected, Patty spent much of her time on the phone. While she jabbered on and on, she would toss forbidden foods she had smuggled in—Twinkies, Baby Ruths, and what not—to my daughter.

". . . If I can just keep her mouth full maybe she'll shut up. God can this kid talk. . . . She loves her sugar, this girl;

you can tell she doesn't get enough of it. . . . No, he's a weirdo about food, a real health nut . . . yeah, fish and Oriental stuff and I don't know what all."

Judging from the chime of the mantel clock, she spent an entire two hours on the phone. At one time Violet asked her to get off and help with the lock on the back door.

"I said shut up, Violet! Sheez, this kid's gonna drive me crazy . . . Here. Have a Butterfinger and leave me alone."

Violet persisted.

"Violet, you're a pain in my ass, a pain in my ass!"

"I am not," she replied. "My daddy says I'm a good, sweet girl."

"Well your daddy doesn't know anything. You're a brat."

Sometime around noon, I heard Patty answer the door and lead her convict boyfriend, Bobby, into the kitchen.

"Just don't touch nothin' because he'll know if you do."

"Yeah, yeah, babe."

"Violet! Violet! Get in here. . . . I'm goin' out for a while, and Bobby here is gonna take care of you, okay?"

"Where are you going?" Violet asked.

"Where am I going? You're as nosy as your poppa. I'm going with Nancy to the flea market, Miss Smarty Pants, and don't tell your daddy. If you tell your daddy I'm not gonna bring you no more treats, okay?"

At this point I also could hear Jo's voice in my head, advising me to calm down, not to overreact. I got up to get a glass of water then sat down to listen to part two: The Convict and Violet.

Of course, he immediately made a phone call.

"It's Bobby," he said. "Yeah . . . all but one bag . . . No, you bring it here to me, I want my cash now. . . . I don't know, some house down on Quail Run something, Quail Run Drive. No, no. Down by the canal. It's got a fuckin' red door, big house, you can't miss it. Yeah, they got some money. . . . No, no, they're not here. I'm alone. . . . And I want all of it this time, okay, Randy? Okay?"

I slammed the recorder on the table so hard the batteries shot out of their cylindrical compartment like missiles, landed on the floor then quickly rolled underneath the refrigerator as if to flee from my anger.

"I'm gonna kill you, Patty Baumgardner!" I yelled. I stood up and called Jo, pulling her out of a meeting.

"Relax and slow down, Lincoln," Jo said. "Are you exaggerating? Maybe just a little?"

"Then you listen to it! She's verbally abusing and poisoning our daughter."

"I don't think Twinkies are poison."

"Jo!"

"I'm only trying to be the calm voice of reason here. You're a hothead, and you don't like her. Are you being fair?"

"Okay, then how do you like this one: Patty's sweet little boyfriend is dealing drugs from our house."

"Someone came to the house?"

"Yes."

"To buy drugs from Patty's boyfriend?"

"Yes."

"Are you sure?"

"Yes."

"That's grounds for firing."

"Thank you."

"Whatever you do, don't tell her you taped her. It's against the law in New York."

"So what do I say?"

"Just tell her our situation has changed and we no longer will be needing her services. And give her a severance. I think two weeks' pay is standard in a situation like this."

"I'm not paying her a goddamn thing!"

"You want her to sue us? She will, Lincoln, she fits the profile. So pay her."

I love my wife's unflappable nature. It is the pole I hold onto in times of high wind, the storms of my heart and mind. I knew I probably should wait until the morning, after calming down, but sleep would not come until I'd finished the job. I am compulsive; I know, I cannot leave anything undone. It's why I could never be a sculptor or painter, dabbing or chiseling day after day, not knowing when the work would be finished until the very last second, and maybe not even then. If I see a spot on the wood floor that I missed vacuuming, I will pull out and assemble the entire in-house vac just to suck up that one fist-sized spot of dust. Similarly, I needed to clean Patty out of our lives.

I dialed her number. She answered on the first ring. I was so mad I trembled, and the words tumbled out pell-

mell, like an overturned bowl of marbles cascading down a
flight of stairs.

"You're fired Patty and I don't want to see your face
ever again."

"What do you mean fired? Linc? Is that you?"

"Fired," I said. "I want your ass gone. Don't even
bother coming in tomorrow."

"What? What the frick? What for?" she asked.

"Never mind," I said. "You're lucky I haven't killed you
yet."

"You're frickin' crazy, ya know that?"

I hung up on her and slapped the counter with both
hands, causing the phone to fall from its cradle on the wall.
The kitchen was a mess. I'd peeled potatoes to make a
Latin shepherd's pie, something of my own creation that
included chorizo and potatoes infused with cumin, garlic
and chipotle peppers, all topped with queso blanco and
homemade pico de gallo.

Still so mad I was shaking, I flipped on the garbage disposal then imagined the peelings to be Patty, and this is
how I would like to dispose of her after I've slowly, tortur-
ously killed her, body part by body part crammed through
that molded rubber opening, then shredded and minced
and flushed down the sewer to be with her own kind.

Maybe I would see her crossing a street in Pittsford and
witness her getting run over by a car, and she would be lying there, semiconscious, and I would walk up to her, and
she would say, "Linc, thank God you're here," and I would

smile and continue across the street, into the store to buy my groceries because no one harms my family and gets away with it. Justice must be served. This is my fantasy. I will keep it to myself.

Date: Sat. 6 April

From: ReadSiouxFalls@pdi.dakota.gov

To: LincolnM@aol.com

You know I like surprises, and Sioux Falls has dropped a big one on me. . . . there's an authentic-sized David (as in Michelangelo) standing on the river in a park here, towering over the water like a lighthouse. Funny thing, though: Evidently there was a cry of horror when the naked man was erected (sorry, couldn't resist), so they turned him with his bum to the park so his more objectionable pecker faced the water. Probably best anyhow, the curves of an athletic man's shapely butt are far more beautiful—and easier to sketch—than that tangled mass up front. Which leads me to my newest confession. . . . .

I met the most engaging woman the other night. She's the owner of a gallery on main street here, and I sold her two charcoal landscapes of the Badlands. She gave me a tour of the city, including the new artists' co-op, then fixed me a meal of lamb shanks and saffron potatoes. I think I loved her house the most, Lincoln. . . . her yard filled with sculptures from different artists, homemade candles on every tabletop, a collection of fabulous antique quilts that I'll tell you about later. This is why

she was so sexy: She listened to me, REALLY listened to
me, was fascinated by my travels and my life and every-
thing I had to say. I've never seen anyone listen with
such attention, rapt, and her eyes never stopped prob-
ing, and every time I looked at her I felt as if they were
deep holes, very much like Mark Rothko paintings, and
if I stepped up to them and looked any closer I would
fall in. She asked. And then I chickened out. And I'm
still mad at myself for not doing it.

. . . . . I'm mad because it shows I'm as set in my
ways as your father. Mad because I'm not able to leap
into another life as easily as I think I could. Mad
because now I must face the fact that we all. . . . ad-
ults, anyway . . . find our niche of comfort and do not
stray. . . . and occasional flirting with different life-
styles and interests is simply a vacation from nor-
malcy. . . . . we all have a place where we belong; I
just happened to choose the wrong place, but I've been
there so long I would fit in nowhere else.

I'm mad because I've always wanted to know if an-
other woman really does know what another woman
wants, just as Anais Nin alluded.

Oh well. . . . . . So I'm heading off to a place I found
on a map: Last Chance, Colorado. I cannot resist such
bold symbolism.

Mom

This trip of my mother's had grown so absurd it had
ceased to be real in my mind. It seemed more like a televi-

sion show that we periodically tune into. Had I grown too selfish to care? Too bored? Was I still mad at her? Or was it simply because, with this new job, I had no time or energy in my life to think of her?

I signed off and returned to Jo on the couch, where she lay reading some paperwork.

"Another e-mail from Mom," I said.

"Where is she now?" Jo asked.

"South Dakota."

I pushed in some goofy Jim Carrey video and lay down with her, my feet at her head and vice-versa, what we call the couch-potato-sixty-nine position, necessary because, with my broadness, we both cannot squeeze our torsos onto the same side.

I heard the clomping of Violet's feet on the deck, then the whisper of the sliding glass door opening.

"Daddy?" she asked.

"Yes, honey."

"Can I have barrettes?"

"Barrettes?"

"Sarah has barrettes, and I want barrettes."

"Don't you mean, 'May I have barrettes, please?'"

"Please."

"The whole thing over again, please."

"Can I have barrettes, please?"

"You never wear barrettes."

"Please, Daddy."

"Okay, sweetie. Go get me the hair brush."

As Violet scampered down the hall and up the stairs, I noted the look of sad resignation on Jo's face.

"Honey . . ."

"She interacts more with the damn cat than she does with me."

Though she'd been home all day, Jo had largely been ignored by Violet. She still came to me for everything, asking me for a Band-Aid, me to cut her chicken at lunch, me to cut out a paper doll of Princess Di.

"You're never here, Jo. She's used to coming to me for things."

"I know, I know, but that doesn't make me feel any better."

"You'd go crazy at home, you know that."

"I'm not so sure."

"You'd go nuts. You think you could play make-believe with fairy dolls for an hour?"

"You do that?"

"Yes, I do that."

Jo shifted her body and sat up so she could look me in the eyes.

"I know I shouldn't be, but sometimes I'm jealous of the time you've had with her," she said.

"Of me?"

"And then the other part of me is glad you've been home because you're so good with her. I don't have to worry about her, Lincoln. That's a huge relief for me. I wish you liked staying home."

"Why?"

"Things get done."

"I've got to go to the bathroom," I said.

I found Violet upstairs, scavenging for barrettes in her toy drawer.

"You know, honey, your Mommy is so good with hair. Wouldn't you like her to brush your hair and snap in your barrettes in a very special way that only mommies can do?"

"No, Daddy, I want to play. Mommy will take too long."

I feigned an attempt with one barrette then stopped. "I'm not too good at this. See? Why don't you go tell Mommy that you want her to fix up your hair."

Silence. I could tell she was walking the fence, preparing to jump on the side where I did not want her to land.

"I tell you what . . . Mommy loves Madeline. Why don't you go put on the video about when Madeline finds the dog and you can sit and watch together and she can fix your hair. Then you can go back outside."

"Please fix my barrettes, Daddy."

"No, Violet, I won't."

She looked up at me, surprised. I crouched down to her level and squeezed her shoulders. I love her little shoulders, how they feel so tiny in my hands, like the meaty ends of raw chicken legs.

"I'm asking you to do me a favor. I do favors for you all the time. I cook for you and play with you and take you to the park. People in a family do things for each other. Now

you do this for me. Go ask your mother to fix these barrettes. Please."

"Yes, Daddy."

"And do not tell her I said this."

I heard her yelling to Jo as she walked down the stairs,
the barrette pinched in a way that made her look as if she
had a tiny fountain spewing from her head. "Mommy, look
what Daddy did! Can you fix this?"

They were on the couch, together, when the phone
rang. I got up to answer.

"Lincoln?"

"Mom?"

"Yes."

"Where are you?"

"I'm in Colorado, like I told you I'd be."

I'd neglected to read the date of the last e-mail. It could
have been a week old. I hadn't been logging on as often as I
used to. No time, and I wasn't as lonely and needy for con-
nections as I used to be.

"Are you okay?" I asked.

"Lincoln, I wrecked my car. I wrecked my beautiful car.
I'm okay, but my car's not."

"What happened?"

"I'd parked it on a little highway beside an abandoned
Stuckey's—remember Stuckey's?—and I hiked across this
meadow, over to a windmill I wanted to sketch, and I heard
a terrible sound. I looked back, and a truck had caught the
edge of it. I don't think I parked it far enough off the road."

"How bad is it?" I asked.

"Oh, it's gone, honey. The engine block looks like a crushed Coke can. But the truck driver was very sweet. He stayed with me the whole time and even bought me dinner in Wray. That's a town here. It's where I am now."

She paused; I waited, not knowing the direction she hoped this conversation would take.

"Lincoln?" she asked.

"Yeah?"

"What should I do?"

"What do you want to do, Mom?"

"I want to bury my poor car. I just can't leave her here."

I'd paced out to the kitchen, and I sat down at the table in the dark, remembering all the things my mother never could leave alone. We replaced dishes or flatware only when there were two or three stragglers left behind, and they stayed on even after the replacements came aboard, and my mother always reached for the older ones first, as if to remind them they were favorites, not members of a vanishing breed. I remembered eating stale Cheerios because she said it wasn't fair for the hangers-on to get tossed in the trash simply because of their position in life, at the bottom of the box. I remembered old shoes and how my mother would fill them with concrete and lay them in the trunk of the car in winter so she would have traction in the snow. Everything in our house got a second life, a second chance. This pleased my father because he thought she was being thrifty. I knew otherwise. I knew my mother was incapable of abandonment.

"Mom," I said. "You can't find a second home for a car. It's too big."

"Well I'm going to, and I won't come home until I do. Josh said he's going to help me."

"Josh . . ."

"My truck driver."

"Mom, please be careful."

"Lincoln, he's a eunuch from the Vietnam War. He's not going to hurt me. He likes me. Don't he like your father. It is possible to like someone of the opposite sex as a friend."

"And then are you going home?"

"Do you think I should?" she asked.

"That's your decision, Mom."

"Do you think your dad will be mad at me?"

"I think you're his sole entertainment in life, Mom. I think he misses you."

"Has he said that?"

"No. But it's obvious to me."

"I thought so. I'd be happier if he would just talk to me, just say something interesting and deep and sweet once in a while. Why can't he express himself like you?"

There was no doubt my mother had done everything she could to mold me into her idea of a perfect husband, and it is a strange feeling indeed when you realize your own mom would rather be married to you than to your dad. Still, I was grateful for all the female-supremacy in-doctrination, learning early on how to appreciate and con-nect with women. Without my mother's influence, I would have surely gone mad this past year. I must admit I have not missed the friendship of men. Men are like a row of dwarf junipers, forever green, forever solid, erect and predictable, growing taller without reaching out to intertwine with others, genetically destined to reach a certain height and no more. Women are sprawling gardens, a cacophonous mixture of annuals and perennials that climb and twist and stretch, everything interwoven and complex, beauty in chaos that alternates between barren and lush.

"What should I do?" she asked.

"Call him, Mom. Just call him."

"You're quiet this morning Linc," Nan said, as we crested the hill at the top of Saddle Creek Run.

"I know what it is," Joanne said. "You're constructing the day in your mind, and you're wondering how you're going to get it all done."

"Bingo," I said.

"What are you doing for day care?" Nan asked.

"I'd be dying without the baby-sitters from the college," I said. "And thanks for helping me out yesterday, Joanne."

"Your daughter's a joy," she said. "Anytime. Really, Linc, it's no problem."

Yet my silence, truth be known, was more related to pouting. That previous night, before going to bed, I logged on to get my e-mail and discovered a letter Nan had sent me by mistake, one originally addressed to "the girls." It was one of those long e-mails in which everyone adds a comment on the bottom then passes it on, bouncing from mom to mom over the past week. As I read the chain letter, I felt like a boy hiding under the bed at a college girls' slumber party. They talked about how fall was coming and how it made them depressed, and how PMS is the absolute bottom of the dark well. They talked about eating a carton of Häagen-Dazs rum raisin ice cream and an entire bag of Cape Cod potato chips. They talked about the clothes at the Gap and how everything was brown this year, and how that was so depressing. They talked of how they cried—*cried!*—when they saw the picture in the *Democrat and Chronicle* of the ancient oak tree in the village square that was dying because someone had poured chemicals at the drip line. Obviously, hormones and the death of green life were getting them down.

I felt betrayed. I thought I'd been brought into the loop. Yet I'd always suspected that women have a secret society, and when they talk in private, away from men, they drop another two or three barriers. I could share with these women—surely they knew that by now—but theirs was a private club, created by hormonal-behavioral differences and a long history of male dominance, and I could not cross those barriers. Though I shared their struggles and day-to-day worries, I was not invited.

I worked from my office at home as much as possible because that meant I would not need a baby-sitter. In between projects and meals and little child-related emergencies, I started to winnow through the twenty-two responses we'd received from our nanny-wanted classified in the *Democrat and Chronicle*. I had just interviewed number one—thumbs down, by the way—when I walked through the kitchen and smelled something rotten.

It was on top of the stove, a pan of black beans I'd let sit for too long. Four days too long. They had begun to smell like the toe jam in dirty winter-time feet, when all those dead skin cells and material fibers and sweat ferment all day in darkened shoe caves. In retrospect, I know I should have thrown them in the trash, but instead I started pushing them down the garbage disposal, which quickly stopped up.

"Shit!"

At five-fifteen, Jo walked into the house with Meredith, one of our baby-sitters. I was on the floor beneath the kitchen sink, unclogging the drain.

"Hi, Mr. Menner," Meredith said.

"I'm taking you out for dinner," Jo said.

"Why?" I asked, retightening the goose neck in the pipe.

"To thank you for everything you do around here."

We chose to eat at Nada, a new Mexican fusion restaurant downtown on Monroe Avenue. Wanting to feel childless and hip and young, I dressed in a black long-sleeve shirt and black jeans and my bolo tie made of a turquoise saguaro cactus. I hadn't had a chance to wear the jeans yet; they were the first thirty-six waist I'd fit into in little more than a year. I stood in front of the bathroom mirror and admired myself. I'd lost fourteen pounds, the gut substantially deflated.

Everything fell into place for a great evening. Jo was in a bright mood, happy about something, probably work, but that was okay as long as the gaiety bled into my life as well. My entrée was surprising and hearty, a ginger-heavy stir-fry of rabbit and winter vegetables wrapped in a seaweed tortilla. We talked about summer camps and Violet's teacher, and we planned vacations for the next year. Intuitively, I knew Jo had another agenda item for the evening. She had not been drinking much wine, and I know she prefers to be lucid when dispensing news that has the potential to knock me off balance.

Though Marilyn had once implied that Jo was having an affair—"You don't think she's working all that time, do you?"—I'd eliminated that possibility long ago. When you're home all day with no adults, your paranoias run wild, unchecked and unchallenged—"Do you love me, honey? Are you mad at me?"—and they metamorphose into monsters. I never used to second-guess my emotions as much as I do now. Still, I'd learned that it is impossible to keep such secrets from whoever does the housework. I would know if she were being unfaithful. I would see it in the self-conscious way she changes into her nightgown, I would smell another man on her clothes. I would note an unfamiliar name in her Day-Timer or find the restaurant or hotel receipt thrown underneath the car seat, which she unconsciously uses as a wastebasket. I know this house and the habits of the occupants as well as the whisker patterns on my face. It is I who cleans under the beds and empties the pockets and searches inch by inch for the missing earring or sock or contact lens or Barbie shoe.

I refilled my wineglass and replaced the bottle into the sweating, copper bucket.

"Okay, honey," I said. "Lay it on me. What is it?"

She looked at me, cocking her head as if to adjust her vision. She does the same thing some mornings when looking in the mirror, when she's trying on something that doesn't fit very well or is a bad color match. She then lay down her fork and knife and reached across the table for my hands.

"I'm a little worried about your reaction."

"Try me. . . . No, let me guess. A transfer. We're moving."

She shook her head.

"A promotion."

"No. . . . Linc, I'm . . ."

I had ruled out an affair, I had ruled out cancer (She was too happy this evening), I had ruled out anything to do with her job. With a life so consumed with work and no time to develop much of anything personal, there was only one possible sentence that such a serious "I'm" could begin. This would explain her slower pace in the morning these past few weeks. It would explain what had been an inexplicable and uncharacteristic peacefulness I'd been seeing on her face at night when she slept. It would explain the hot tea replacing wine. There had been the thin veil of a good secret hanging between us these past few weeks, and I had wondered, in fact worried, what it might have been.

"You're pregnant."

She nodded.

"Is that okay?" she asked.

There was a time two months back, six months back, a year back when the news would have kicked me off a cliff, yet over this past year the little machine in my brain that spits out emotions had undergone vast renovation. I rarely feel cleanly segmented emotions anymore. Everything nowadays comes out complex and bundled and interconnected because it is just not my emotions under consideration but also those of every person under my care, and it can therefore take me hours, sometimes days, to understand my reaction to something. I was frightened and happy for myself, frightened and happy and relieved for Jo, frightened and curious and optimistic about the impact a sibling would have on Violet.

"I knew we weren't being careful enough," I said.

"Oh, God," Jo said. "That means you're unhappy."

"No. It means I need to practice better self-control when it comes time to putting on a rubber."

I smiled, and she smiled in return.

"This is a good time," I said. "We need to find a new nanny, but this is a good time."

We left the restaurant and walked home, saying very little, holding hands the entire way. Meredith and Violet would not return until after ten. There was an ice-cream social at Meredith's dorm, and Violet had wanted to go with her.

When we opened the door from the garage, I could tell with my nose that something was amiss, not as we had left things. I smelled chlorophyll and . . . soil. We walked into the kitchen and turned on the light.

"Oh my God," Jo gasped. "*Passiflora!*"

All sixty feet of it had been yanked from its lofty home near the ceiling, and she was lying like a rope in a pile in the middle of the kitchen floor, slashed with a paring knife from the roots and the pot she'd occupied for a year. We walked up to it slowly. I reached down and gently picked up a section of it, holding it in my hands as if it were a dead snake.

"Oh, man!" I whined. "I forgot to re-tumble the locks."

I walked over to the phone and pounded out Patty's number. One ring, two, four, six, finally her answering machine, though I knew damn well she was home. Yet I hung up after the beep, recording nothing, the moment lost, the passion and anger now back down to a simmer. I looked at *passiflora*, who, like streamers ripped down after a party, had lost her significance and beauty.

Genesee Hospital not only made budget for the year but also out-performed all hospitals in the company's east-coast division. To celebrate, Jo rented out the entire Rochester Children's Museum for an evening and invited every division director, their direct reports as well, and all of their families.

Jo had told me she could take Violet herself, that I didn't need to go, yet in my mind I did not have a choice. I had snubbed most hospital-related spouse command appearances over the past year, and I still needed to meet the people who were so important to my wife at work.

On a hunch, I called the caterer ahead of time to find out what he was serving that night. Jo's assistant, who sets these things up, does not have children, and she is not sensitive to their needs. When I learned that the menu was going to be tuna sushi, Caesar salad and a spicy tomato-based pasta called chicken diablo, I decided I would cook up a huge mess of macaroni and cheese for the kids and bring it along. Without telling Jo, I also bought Parker fountain pens engraved with "Genesee No. 1" for her direct reports.

Hokey as it may sound, I was happy and proud standing beside my wife all evening. Jo was beautiful in a beige cashmere turtleneck and the earrings I'd bought her for Mother's Day, a pair of sleeping bronze suns. I had dressed up in my navy blazer and chinos and the orange-and-blue tie covered in children's stick-figure people. Though she had come to play, I still put Violet in a knee-length, hibiscus-red dress. We had gone out and bought black, patent-leather shoes especially for the event.

Few of these people knew of my new job, most of them thought I was still at home full time, and I didn't bother correcting them because it really didn't matter in this situation. Three or four people remembered seeing my picture in the *Sun*, the weekly suburban rag in Pittsford that runs what I call micro news: school lunch menus, Rotary club highlights, photographs of marriages, golfers who hit a hole in one. Earlier in the year, a reporter had heard about my houseplants—a jungle, she called it—and wanted to take a look. Though I'd steadily been buying green tropicals, I was surprised at how many I had. The reporter, a young woman named April, counted one hundred and six, most of them on the first floor of the house, and they wanted to come take a picture. For the photograph, I posed with Violet in a corner of ferns and my passion flower vine. The headline over the photo said "Pittsford's Plant Man." The caption beneath was even more insipid. It referred to me as Mr. Mom and told readers that Jo was the COO of Genesee Memorial. The reporter said nothing about my landscaping expertise, only that I've "always had a passion for plants."

My reaction back then, five months ago, was very different from what it would be today. I was instantly upset because they made me sound like some flaming interior decorator. I thought all day about calling to raise hell, but what would I say? That she neglected to mention what I used to be out in the real world? That I was landscaper to the stars? That my work had been seen on *Lifestyles of the Rich and Famous*? She made me sound shallow and unimportant and coddled and kept, though to an outsider I suppose it did look that way.

Jo and I decided to spend two vacation days finding a nanny. This time we interviewed the final five in our home, all one after the other. We started at eight in the morning and finished some time after six. I'd never seen Jo interview before; I was surprised anyone even wanted the job when she was done with them. Secretly timing each candidate, she threw out situation scenarios to each and asked them to react. She had them take phone messages and read to Violet and take a test on first aid. She asked them to describe their children, if applicable, and marriages or relationships. Of course I approved of her technique.

That night, as we ate a white pizza from Bantoni's, we discussed our options, which were slim.

"I liked the Balkan grandma," I said. "She's simple, but I like her heart. She makes me feel good."

"But she flunked her first aid," Jo said. "You can't base this solely on intuition, Lincoln. You did that before and got Patty."

"Then which one did you like?" I asked.

She reached for the clear plastic cup of red sauce and poured some over her pizza, which she ate with a fork. "Honestly? None of them."

"How can you say that? You've got to pick one."

Jo's beeper vibrated at her hip. She reached down, pressed a button and read the display.

"All I know, Lincoln, is that not one of those women

would spend the time that you spend developing Violet's intellect. What we have here is a group of baby-sitters, not intuitive teachers, and I want both in one package."

"You're not going to find it," I said.

"We will because we demand it."

"We're not going through this whole process again, Jo. We don't have time. I have to find somebody."

The phone rang. I heard Violet running to answer. "Let me get it, let me get it!" Prompted by the sullen and mumbling "hello" that Nan's sons utter when answering the telephone, I'd decided to work with Violet on phone manners, and she grabbed at each possible chance to show how well she could do.

"Hello, this is the Menners, Violet speaking. . . . Grammy! Grammy, are you home?"

I had shared with Violet edited highlights from my mother's adventure, making it sound like a vacation, which, in some ways, was true. I do not like to hide things from my daughter, especially those matters, such as a disappearing grandmother, that affect her. So many mothers forget what it's like to be a kid, that a child listens to every adult-whispered word possible because they realize that everything, ultimately, will affect them in some way. I have discovered that if I'm honest and straightforward with Violet then she generally treats me with the same respect.

I let Violet have her say then broke into the conversation to let them know I'd gotten on another phone.

"Lincoln!" said Dad, more ebullient than I'd ever heard him. "It's your father—and your mother."

"Hello, sweetheart," she said.

"When did you pull in?" I asked.

"Late last night," answered Dad.

What else could I say in such a situation? How was your trip? Do you like your husband anymore? What plans do you have for the future? I knew that my father would not want to talk about it, that having Mom gone was like having a dirty showroom floor at the dealership, and now she was back, and the floor was cleaned and waxed; and the scuff marks forgotten. Theirs is a hugely dysfunctional relationship, one of those with few actual eruptions. Rather, the lava churns and roils inside, unsuccessfully looking for an exit, until it finally cools off and hardens, building another impenetrable layer. I knew for almost certain that this trip of my mother's might never be discussed.

"Aren't you going to tell him about your surprise?" he asked. "Tell him what I got you, Carol."

"Your father got me a new car," she said.

"What happened to yours?" I asked, not knowing what she'd told him.

"Some asshole stole it," he interjected. "Town Cars are high on the hit list. . . . I got her the same car she had. . . . The same exact car, didn't I, honey?"

"The same exact car," Mom said. I could sense sarcasm in her tone.

"It took some work," he said. "But I finally found one, same Mediterranean Royale Blue. A dealer in Modesto, he had one."

"What are your plans now, Mom?" Though it sounded

like a slightly veiled insult—"Please tell us if you plan on running away again."—I did not intend it to be.

"No plans." She was very quiet, seemingly trying to avoid participation in this conversation, no doubt for the same reason someone avoids his friends after a drunken evening when too much is done, too much is said. For a time, embarrassment rises up like bitter vomit.

"It was quite a trip, but I think she's done with traveling for a while," Dad said. He sounded bouncy and giddy, like a child whose lost dog, long taken for dead, had just come home.

I could picture her pouting in the passive way that goes undetected by my father. I hoped she would accept the car for what it was, a peace offering from a man who wasn't quite sure just why he had to make such an offer.

"You sound happy," said Mom. "Are you happy?"

"I'm happy, overwhelmed but happy."

"Sometimes being overwhelmed is good," she said. "You can't get bored when you're overwhelmed."

"And soon to be even more overwhelmed."

"What do you mean?"

"Jo's pregnant."

"Lincoln! I thought you just wanted one."

"Well, we're having two."

"How do you feel about that?"

I cut the conversation short. I was certain she could sense the coolness in my voice, though the source of the displeasure would not be detected because even I was not sure why I was mad. My feelings toward my mother were as complex as my thirty-two-ingredient recipe for jerk seasoning, obvious heat and anger on the end but created by a swirling mélange of flavors that simultaneously fight and embrace one another. I was mad at her escapist, low-resistance ways, mad for her not being there when I needed her most, mad at her for selfishly putting herself in danger when her family could not help. Yet I was envious and respectful of her courage and the dramatic style in which she had pursued happiness.

The man in me rolled my eyes. The woman in me cheered her on. I am both of these now.

Jo had business in Nashville all week long, and instead of frantically juggling work and Violet I decided to take five sick days. I had forgotten how much more leisurely even grocery shopping could be when I had no one else pulling on my chain. I had time to interact with Violet on her level and to cook the things I wanted to cook.

"What are these?" the cashier asked me, holding the plastic sack of fruit aloft.

"Pomegranates," I said.

"What you gonna do with 'em?"

"I'm using them on a salad."

"What kind?"

"I'm roasting poblano chilies, and then I'm going to toss those with curly endive and the Stilton cheese and the pomegranate seeds . . . and maybe a little tangerine juice . . . and maybe a little toasted cumin. Sort of a Mexican salad."

"Whoooeee!" she blurted. "Girls, we got a man who can cook here! You got a brother? Because I want a man who can cook."

"No brother. Sorry."

"Not as sorry as I am."

As I pushed the cart back to the car, I handed the fruit to Violet.

"Say pomegranate," I said.

"Pomgranite," she replied, stroking the leathery skin.

"What do you think it feels like?"

"Like Mommy's purse."

"Yes, but Mommy's purse is made of leather, and where does leather come from?"

"Pomgranites."

"From cows," I said.

"Cows! Milk comes from cows."

"Leather is cow skin."

"Daddy! No!"

"Yes, that's what leather is. Look at your shoes, honey—they're leather."

"They're white, Daddy."

"But why are they white?"

"Painted white."

"You're my smart girl. And what kind of meat comes from cows?"

"Hamburger!"

"Good. Hamburger's made from beef."

"Hamburger," she said, smelling the pomegranate. "Yum."

We were due to pick up Jo at the airport in half an hour. Violet and I always try to go early because we play a game she calls zoomy rocket, which usually draws some nasty maternal stares. I can break the rules of caregiving more often because I'm a man. People think I'm embarrassed about my situation so they're reluctant to approach and censure me. This gives me an advantage. I used to change Violet's diapers on city sidewalks and on the floors of restaurants. I warmed bottles of juice in my armpits. When a sign prohibits strollers on escalators, I pick up the entire thing with Violet inside and carry it in my arms as if it were a large television. If we're eating ice cream without wet wipes, Violet knows she can clean her sticky, vanilla mouth and hands on the leg of my pants. Sometimes, though, I get into trouble with strangers who think I'm endangering my daughter. Twice I've had mothers pluck her from the top of the monkey bars at Fairport Park. I get the most stares of disapproval, however, at the airport, with zoomy rocket.

The baggage-claim area of Rochester International Airport has a granite floor that is cool and slick as a clean plate. As we wait for Jo's plane to come in, Violet lies on her stomach and says "okayokayokaydaddy—rocket!" I crouch down and with the heel of my hand push her on the fanny, shooting her across the floor like a shuffle-board disc for thirty, sometimes forty feet. There's really no way she could get hurt. At LAX it would be impossible to navigate through the dense, random forest of legs, but Rochester International at nine P.M. is a cool tundra free of obstacles. She can't fall. By putting her on her stomach I've eliminated gravity as a possible villain. Without endangering her, I want to create in my little girl a hunger for unharnessed speed because I want her to catch anything and everything she may ever desire.

Much to Violet's glee, Jo's plane was late—"Again!

Again, Daddy!"—and by the time she arrived the front of Violet's white shirt was a brownish gray, a penguin in reverse.

"Mommy!" Violet yelled, running up to Jo.

Jo let her bag on wheels fall to the floor like a felled tree, and she dropped to her knee, arms open. She was ready to scoop Violet up but instead lost her balance on impact, and the two of them rolled backward, Violet on her mother's stomach.

"Oh, Mommy, that's fun!"

"You've gotten so big," Jo said. "Just in one week."

She looked up at me. "I could have taken a cab home, Lincoln. You didn't need to pick me up."

I offered her a hand, which she accepted. On her feet again, she kissed me.

"But aren't you glad I did?" I asked.

In the airport parking lot, Jo climbed into the back seat with Violet. "Do you mind?" she asked me.

Fifteen minutes later, still driving through the rhythmic islands of amber light on the freeway, I heard the giggles in the back finally die down as Violet fell off to sleep. There was a time when I would have been jealous, even angry about the way Jo can waltz into the scene after being gone for so long, and Violet squeals and laughs with her each time, as if Jo is a long-distance friend who's come to town to play for the afternoon. I remembered the Mother's Day tea at Barnes & Noble, and how I skulked in the magazine section while Violet and her mother nibbled on tiny peanut-butter-and-banana sandwiches. I pouted because I thought it was I who should have been there at Violet's side, because these were my peers, not Jo's, and it was I who had made and understood the sacrifices of mother-hood, and things like Mother's Day teas are the well-deserved and anticipated tiny flecks of sugar found in a sometimes sour soup.

"Thanks for keeping her up this late," Jo said. "This is exactly what I needed."

"She'll be a bear tomorrow," I said.

"But thank you, Lincoln."

I looked in the rearview mirror. Though her eyes were closed, Jo was awake, sitting up straight. I felt so connected to her, though the nature of that connection had metamor-phosed into something different. Being the caregiver had pushed me away, no, *elevated* me in some way. When you nurture full-time you perch yourself up high, away from everyone, to get a better view so as not to miss anything in the big picture, so everyone's needs get met and no one goes away unhappy or hungry or feeling bad about them-selves. Like wisteria on an arbor, I'd wrapped myself around Jo and Violet, seeing all sides from all angles as I wind about, intimate not only with their frailties and fears but simple body functions as well. It is I who cleans up their piss and blood, vomit, shit and hair, the very drop-pings of their humanity, which make their way under my fingernails and probably into the sandwich I will eat for lunch. I know when they hurt, why they hurt, how they hurt, because I am standing above, not only watching but directing, prodding, restraining. For so long I had wanted back down there, with them. I did not want to know this much. It's scary to know this much. It has made me far too vulnerable and far too important in their lives. Yet as I drove my girls through the darkness, toward home, I realized that once you venture this far into other people's souls, it is impossible to retreat. You are inside of them, and you cannot get out. They close themselves around you like morning glories at high noon.

Sometime during the week I had decided, almost subconsciously, that the best place for me at this time in my life, at this time in Violet's life, at this time in Jo's life, was at home, not in the Pittsford village hall. A full-time nanny would get everyone fed, but all those little things that make the difference between living and existing—correcting grammar; explaining a nuance on television; the frivolous purchase of a new pair of *Peanuts* socks; being there to answer the phone and listen about an asshole at the hospital; making the extra grocery-shopping trip to get strawberries for the cereal—all these things would be lost in a new household triage in which basic ingredients of survival overshadow those things that bring lightness and beauty to life.

SALAD WITH ROASTED POBLANOS, STILTON CHEESE AND POMEGRANATE SEEDS

SERVES FOUR

4 poblano chilies
1 cup crumbled Stilton or Maytag blue cheese
Seeds from one pomegranate
Enough salad greens for four people (A good choice is a bag of prepared gourmet lettuces found in the produce section.)

THE DRESSING:
1 teaspoon toasted cumin seeds (To toast, put them in a dry skillet over medium-high heat, stirring occasionally so they don't burn on one side.)
2 teaspoons lime juice
1 cup tangerine or orange juice
2 tablespoons light vegetable oil
3 tablespoons rice vinegar (Choose white-wine vinegar if you want a less sweet dressing.)
Fresh ground black pepper

Whisk all dressing ingredients together. Dressing can be made ahead and refrigerated for a day or two.

Grill or broil chilies, blackening them on each side. When finished, wrap the chilies in a paper bag and close for five minutes, helping to loosen the skins. Cut off stems, peel blackened skins off and remove seeds from the chilies. Julienne the chilies.

Toss the chilies, crumbled cheese, dressing, pomegranate seeds and greens.

I could not sleep, and that was okay because there was plenty of laundry to do. In between loads I logged on to check my e-mail and the weather for tomorrow, also to search for children's history books about the Erie Canal and canals in general because I was planning an educational boat trip for some time in the coming year.

Awaiting me was a message from my mother, who always types the words "pertinent information" in the subject space, as if she's afraid her message will get zapped into oblivion before being read.

Date: Wed. 9 May
From: CMenner@aol.com
To: LincolnM@aol.com
For your ears/eyes only here's what happened: I could not leave her in a salvage yard. I had to bury her. So Josh—my trucker friend?—and I towed her out to a lake outside St. Francis, Kansas, a place named Square Lake, though it was actually more of a pear shape. . . . . . and we set her in neutral and pushed her in, and I watched her slip into the gray-green water, out of this vibrant, colorful world and into another.

But something awful happened. With just a foot left, she stopped. Jutting from the water, like some ice jamb in springtime, was a triangle of blue and chrome with a red tail light that looked like a spot of fresh blood. I stripped off my pants and waded out to her, and I grabbed that corner and pulled myself up, hoping I'd pull her under and finish the job. It reminded me of the awful time I tried to put Tippy to sleep with chloroform and didn't quite use enough. She wouldn't budge . . . the lake was too goddamned shallow, and I had to leave her. Exposed like that.

I made Josh wait so I could sketch her. I've painted it. Obviously, because I cannot reveal what it is, every-one thinks it's an abstract, not a portrait of a beloved corpse or an exquisite symbol of my life. By the way, considering all my paintings from the trip, your father has started telling people I went on an artistic sabbati-cal, and that it was a helluva lot cheaper than going to France. Ha, ha. Ha. Very funny.

Why don't you call? Why don't I call? Maybe I grew too accustomed to one-way communication with you. Maybe I'm afraid of your strong judgment and attitude and afraid of what you'll tell me about me and my marriage and my follies. I'm a little embarrassed by it all, really. . . . I grew weary of being a good girl. Don't you grow weary of being a good boy? When will you fall, Lincoln? I keep waiting, watching. Don't fall. Please. I don't recommend it. Mom

When will you fall, Lincoln?

Which made me think of harvesting trees.

Which reminded me: *The pilgrims' harvest.*

Which reminded me: *Be sure to spray sweet corn for weevils this year.*

Should I invite my parents for Thanksgiving?

Should Violet start leading grace?

Find church for family.

Moral decay.

Replace rotten wood around back kitchen window.

The dryer buzzed, alerting me that the yellow load was warm and ready to fold. I looked at my watch—two-thirty—and decided I had time for a red load, but that would be it for tonight. Then tomorrow, a blue load, and the gentle-cycle load of bras and silk nighties, and then the tans and browns and then the bedsheets.

I carried the basket of clothes out onto the back deck so I could fold them in the cool air. It appeared that the only neighbors awake at this hour were myself and Beth Hartwick, who stood engrossed in a task at her kitchen sink. I'd seen her many times before during my late-night walks. Walking at night is the finest form of entertainment, it is channel-surfing, lit window after lit window, rectangles of human activity in full color, all with the mute button on. It amazes me how these people think I can't see them because they can't see me. Though a few men do the dishes, it's usually women I see in the kitchen window over the sink. Their heads are down, eyes focused on something below, their faces serene as a garden pond. They remind me of Madonnas in medieval paintings, only instead of gazing down at Jesus they're looking at dirty dishes in a sink of soap suds. I know what this is about. We find comfort in this nightly moment of solitude. It is when we perform our postmortem of the day, the week, our lives, remembering things to do and things that should have been.

As I folded one of Violet's yellow skirts, I thought of my mother and myself and of how we all fall into long-standing patterns of behavior, occasionally by choice, most often out of necessity, and we break free from those patterns only after a series of random phrases or acts that startle or frighten or anger us in some way. We then get diverted, pushed in a new direction, and we start walking and exploring all over again.

A white Lexus drove by. The Robinsons' terrier barked. I added cat litter to the grocery list in my mind.